BAREFOOT BRIDE FOR THREE

Bride Train 1

Reece Butler

MENAGE EVERLASTING

Siren Publishing, Inc.
www.SirenPublishing.com

A SIREN PUBLISHING BOOK
IMPRINT: Ménage Everlasting

BAREFOOT BRIDE FOR THREE
Copyright © 2010 by Reece Butler

ISBN-10: 1-61034-118-X
ISBN-13: 978-1-61034-118-9

First Printing: November 2010

Cover design by *Les Byerley*
All cover art and logo copyright © 2010 by Siren Publishing, Inc.

Printed in the U.S.A.

PUBLISHER
Siren Publishing, Inc.
www.SirenPublishing.com

DEDICATION

To my favorite three men: Paul, Andy and David.

Please note this is a work of fiction. The town of Tanner's Ford and all but one character appearing in this work were created by me. While Henry Plummer did serve as sheriff of Bannack City, Montana, he did so a few years before the fictional events described in this work took place. Any errors, historical or otherwise, are my own.

BAREFOOT BRIDE FOR THREE

Bride Train 1

REECE BUTLER
Copyright © 2010

Chapter One

Montana Territory, 1870

"Another step and I'll shoot."

Trace Elliott brought his tired horse to an abrupt stop. The beast twitched his right ear, the white one matching the blotches splashed over him like paint. The full moon lit the Colt pointed at Trace's heart. His tense muscles eased when it also glinted off the six-pointed silver star.

"Evening, Sheriff."

"You got a short memory, son." Frank Chambers stood braced for battle with legs wide.

With his attention on the bright lights and action at the far end of town, Trace hadn't seen the man step out from between the mercantile and bank.

"You got the draw on me." Trace shook his head. "Been a long time."

"Only a damn fool or an Elliott would ride a spotted horse into my town on a full moon. One of these days someone will shoot you right out of the saddle."

"I want grub, a hot bath, whiskey, and a woman. I don't mean to cause a ruckus."

Trace scratched at his days-long beard with his left hand. He kept the right one still and in plain view. He thought they had an understanding but the lawman took his job too seriously as far as Trace was concerned. In his book, enjoying a good fight with land-raping miners was a good thing.

"You boys never do. But you still end up fist-deep in a swarm of miners."

"We paid for the saloon window."

"I told you before freeze-up there'd be no Elliotts in my town 'til one of you gets hitched and settles the lot of you down." The sheriff turned his head and spat in the dirt to the side of Trace's horse. "Found a wife yet?"

Trace sighed and resettled his hat. "Gave up looking long ago." His horse shuffled uneasily, and he settled the gelding. "If a decent woman ever made it to this town, she sure as hell wouldn't want me."

"Just so happens I got a bride for you."

Trace narrowed his eyes at the lawman's slow smile. Pa said when a lawman holding a gun showed his teeth, something bad always happened.

"I locked her up a couple days ago," continued Frank. "Mayor Rivers wants her married by midnight. Might as well be you."

Trace idly scratched his chest. A long, cold winter and too few dips in the creek made his skin itch like ants at a picnic. He'd counted on soaking in a hot bath with a whiskey first thing.

Considering the state of things, he could do with a wife. She'd cook, keep the house, clean their clothes, and put up vittles for the winter. Even better, she'd warm his bed during those long, dark nights when wolves and blizzards howled. The good Lord willing, that would lead to children and a future for the Rocking E.

He shifted in the saddle as his body, already eager for what the town offered, hardened further. No more riding into town a couple times a year when the need for a woman got too strong to ignore. He'd learned how to pleasure one long before he turned eighteen. He hadn't had much practice in the seven years since, but some things a man just never forgot.

He'd take the wife. There was no chance a shotgun wedding to an outlaw bride would lead to the foolishness that killed his father. She couldn't be worse than going without. Unless…

"Who'd she kill, Frank?"

"Nobody, yet." Frank slid his gun into its holster. "Arrived Monday from Dillon on the spring Bride Train. Stubborn woman refused every man who asked." He chuckled. "She's your problem now."

"Why'd you lock her up?"

"She's the first woman to ride the Bride Train this far west. She was fine for the first few days but didn't take kindly to a few offers for her favors." He turned toward the jail. Trace followed on his horse. "Big Joe Sheldrake tried to force a kiss on her. She gave him a well-placed knee, then kicked his ass when he bent over, shrieking like a banshee. If I hadn't been across the street, he'd of killed her right there. Once he could straighten up again, that is. I took her boots away and locked her up for being a public nuisance."

"I'd pay gold to see a woman do that to Big Joe."

"You and half the town. No one dares to laugh out loud when he's around, but I've heard a lot of snickers behind his back."

"How long she been in jail?"

"Three days. Mayor Rivers set his hat on the bar at Baldy's Saloon this morning. He'll pick a name at midnight and that's who she'll marry. Big Joe's making sure his name's the only one."

Trace grunted his disapproval. After Big Joe injured one of her girls, he was banned from Miss Lily's Parlor. Supposedly lead hand on the mayor's ranch, Joe spent too little time there for the amount of gold in his pockets. Trace couldn't let the ham-fisted lowlife have a woman with the spunk to stand up for herself. He'd take her even if she was a broken-down hag. Not that he had a choice if he ever wanted to set foot in town again.

"Be a waste of a good woman," continued the sheriff. "I hear she went to one of them Eastern lady's schools, but she also worked on a farm. And she's got spirit."

Trace snorted. "When a man says that about a horse he means it bites, kicks, and bucks."

"She bites and kicks all right. The bucking?" The sheriff winked, man to man. "You'll find that out when you bed her."

"She a looker?"

"She's a woman, Elliott. That's all that matters."

They walked for another minute, Trace keeping his horse to the sheriff's ambling speed.

"What about Simon and Jack?"

"Your brothers can find their own wife, or share yours. Long as she settles you boys down, I don't care who sleeps where." He chuckled. "She's enough of a hellcat, it'll take the three of you to tame her."

Long-denied need shot through Trace. In his experience, women were either meek and honest or devious and full of passion, like the girls working for Lily.

He'd take passion any time. He wanted a wife he didn't have to pussyfoot around, like he'd seen Gillis MacDougal do with the sickly wife he'd found back East. An Elliott woman should roar and fight back rather than weep. And when she fought him, he'd put her across his lap and spank her bare ass. Then he'd kiss it all better and—a feminine shriek erupted from the open door of the nearby jail.

"What the hell was that?"

The sheriff grabbed the startled horse's halter and grinned up at Trace. "Your bride's calling. Go in and say howdy, son. I got a few things to do before you get hitched."

Trace settled his horse, looped his reins over the rail and stepped into the dimly lit jail. The two people in the barred cell were too busy to notice him slide into a dark corner. Charlie, the beefy deputy, held a fistful of light-colored hair. The woman swung her fists, smashing them against Charlie's forearm since she couldn't reach anything else. Trace leaned a shoulder against the wall, ready to move if necessary. He'd see how his wife-to-be handled herself. The parallel scratches across Charlie cheek suggested she wasn't the type to give up without a fight.

The hem of her ugly brown dress moved when she shifted, revealing slim ankles and bare feet. Trace winced when a quick knee just missed landing between the deputy's legs when he shifted at the last moment. Tanner's Ford had never put a woman in jail before. Watching his bride, he understood why the sheriff locked her up. She had spirit, all right.

"Yah cain't fight me, I got a badge!"

"And I've got a brain. That's worth more than a penny's worth of tin!"

Trace smothered his snicker. He stuck his thumbs in his belt, enjoying the action as well as the woman's wit. Ignoring the deputy's grip on her hair, Blondie twisted around and kneed Charlie in his big belly. The man released her with an *oof* and backed off. Long strands of hair trailed from one hand as he covered his gut and fought to breathe. Panting, she grimaced and stood up. She settled her feet shoulder width apart and lifted her fists, waiting for a chance to strike again.

Her hair, damn near to her ass, looked like a packrat's nest. The lamp on the sheriff's desk lit up healthy white teeth bared in a snarl. She was as tall as Charlie, with wide shoulders and hips. The top of her head would reach his nose. Tall for a woman, but just his size.

Tiny women scared the hell out of him. At six foot four in bare feet, he towered over most females. He was afraid he'd hurt one in bed or they'd die from birthing big-headed Elliott babies. This woman was tough enough to travel on her own from the East for a chance at a new life. She'd survived three days in jail and, instead of weeping, she roared like a mountain cat.

She'd be able to handle a ranch and three grown men.

"You hellcat." Charlie rubbed the dirty shirt straining to cover his belly. "You won't be doin' that again. I'm gonna have you right now." He revealed missing teeth when he leered. He took a step toward her. Trace straightened up, arms loose at his sides.

"You'll have to kill me first!"

Blondie darted forward and hit the oaf in the jaw. Charlie, caught taking a step with one foot in the air, staggered and fell back. His back slammed into the thick bars of the cell door and he slid to the floor. She danced around, squawking "ow, ow, ow" and shaking her hand. Charlie, flat on his ass, shook his head like a bear. He glared up at her. She curled her lip at him. He grabbed the bars. Cursing like a muleskinner, he slowly hauled himself to his feet.

"Dammit, Deputy!" yelled the sheriff as he strode past Trace into the jail. "What the hell you doing in there?"

Charlie turned toward the sheriff, still holding on to the bars with one hand. "Showing her how a real man treats a woman!"

"Real man?" shrieked Blondie. "There isn't a real man to be found in this town. And I'm not marrying anything less!"

"Ma'am," said Frank Chambers, "Mayor Orville Rivers says you're to be married by midnight."

"I beg your pardon?" She said it like a demand rather than a question.

"You chose to ride the Bride Train to find a husband," said Sheriff Chambers. Hands on his hips, he spoke calmly, as if they conversed over dinner. "You came all this way without choosing a husband. Tanner's Ford is the end of the line, and you still refused every man who asked. It's out of my hands now." He shrugged. "Mayor says you cause too much trouble."

"Trouble? I merely defended myself from disgusting pigs like him!"

She pointed at Charlie. He growled and lunged toward her. Trace palmed his gun and aimed. The sheriff hauled on the back of Charlie's shirt through the bars, stopping him from moving forward.

"Settle down or you'll stay in this cell until Monday," ordered Frank. "You had your chance to put your name in the hat and get this woman. She's not for you." Charlie shook off the sheriff's hand but didn't move forward.

"What hat?" Trace noted that Blondie's jaw stuck out worse than Simon when Pa refused to buy him a candy stick.

"Ma'am, single women who refuse to marry upset the town wives. They complain to their husbands who then go to the mayor. His job is to fix the problem, and that means getting you married. Since you won't choose a husband, he put his hat on the bar in the saloon this morning. You'll marry the man whose name he pulls out at midnight."

"*What!*"

"You heard me, Miss James. You'll be married tonight come hell or high water."

"This is preposterous!" She grimaced so hard Trace thought she might break a tooth. "Mrs. McLeod said there's hundreds of unmarried men who'd take any kind of wife. Line them up on the street tomorrow and I'll choose one."

The sheriff shook his head. "Too late. Joe Sheldrake put his name in the hat first. No one wants to go against him. He's already celebrating in Baldy's Saloon."

Even in the lantern light with her face covered with dirt, Trace could see the blood drain from Blondie's face. "No," she whispered, shaking her head. "You can't let that beast touch me. He said he'd kill me."

The empty holes in Charlie's mouth showed when he laughed. "Big Joe says I kin watch him learn you to be a wife." He leaned forward and stabbed a thick finger at her. "When he's tired a you, he'll rent you out for whiskey. You'll lift your skirts when a man tells you."

Both Charlie and Blondie jumped at the screech when the sheriff pulled the cell door open. The deputy was so wide he blocked the sheriff from entering. With them in her way, Blondie didn't rush to escape but held her fists at her side, head high and jaw clenched. Her eyes did flick to the open door and back again, as if measuring her chances to squeeze through.

The sheriff turned his head to Trace. He lifted an eyebrow and pointed to Trace and then the woman. He backed out of the cell but only Trace noticed.

"No one hits me and gets away with it," said Charlie.

Trace watched him inhale deep as if enjoying the smell of her fear. Blondie swallowed hard. She didn't look around or plead for help but her whole body trembled. Someone had beaten this woman. Whoever it was, she knew she'd get no help. Yet she'd stood tall and fought back, the pain worth her pride. Trace understood too well. He absently rubbed the scars around his neck.

Eyes on his prize, Charlie took a step and raised his beefy hand. She gulped and raised her fists. Without moving out of the shadowed corner, Trace cracked the hammer back on his gun. The unmistakable snap caught Charlie with right hand raised high. He stopped all movement.

Blondie wasted no time. She hopped on the bed, around the unmoving deputy, and out of the cell. She scurried to the wall behind the sheriff's desk and braced her back against it. She moved her head between the cell and the dark corner where Trace waited.

The lantern on the sheriff's desk lit a slice of enticing white flesh through a rip in her bodice. More skin showed when she hauled air into her substantial chest, spreading the torn fabric. Her waist flared out to woman-sized hips. She could do with a bit of fattening up, but everyone was lean and hungry in the spring.

Her hair must have been blonde when clean. He couldn't tell if she had color under her dirty face and hands, but he hoped she wasn't one to burn easily. Over the years, he'd dreamed of places where he'd take his wife if he ever found one. He'd spread her out on sweet Elliott grass and explore every inch of her in the bright sun. Then he'd make her scream her passion so his name echoed through the valley.

Never had he thought the dream would come true.

"Get out before I take that badge," said Sheriff Chambers to Charlie. The deputy scowled in Trace's direction. He straightened up, spat on the floor, and squinted into the dark corner where Trace waited.

"Who's the coward what drew a gun on me? Yah might as well put a red circle on yer back."

"Shut up," said the sheriff. "You're lucky Trace didn't shoot you right off for lifting your hand to his woman."

"She's Elliott's woman?" Charlie gulped. "Since when?"

"Since now," croaked Trace. He stepped out of the shadows. Charlie's face paled from belligerent red. "No one touches what's mine and lives," said Trace. He holstered his gun, staring hard at Charlie. He gave a sharp jerk of his head in an unspoken order.

Charlie understood the motion and scuttled from the jail, keeping far from Trace on his way to the street. Sheriff Chambers walked over to the woman who would soon become Trace's wife.

"Miss Elizabeth James, this is Trace Elliott. You need a husband to get you out of town, and he needs a wife to let him in."

The woman's high forehead crinkled as if she couldn't understand his words. She brushed strands of loose hair away with a grimace.

"Come say howdy to your fiancé," continued the sheriff. "You got a few minutes to get to know each other while I haul the preacher out of Baldy's Saloon." His boots thumped across the quiet jail. He stopped a few feet from the door and turned back.

"Don't worry, ma'am. You wanted a real man for a husband, and you found one. Nobody in Montana Territory messes with an Elliott." He nodded and closed the door behind him.

Trace rolled his shoulders and sighed. If he and his twin brothers were so good, why had the sheriff banned them from town? His stomach grumbled. One look at the burned beans Jack called supper and he'd headed to town for one of Sophie's hot suppers. The hotel did a raging business as there was nowhere closer than Bannack City where a single man could get a decent meal.

Now what? With Ma dead for seven years, most of what he knew of females came from Miss Lily's experienced gals.

What the hell could he say to a smart-talking, Eastern virgin?

Chapter Two

Elizabeth James pressed her back against the cold jail wall. The stone, solid and sturdy, helped to steady her. A few months ago she'd thought marrying old Mr. Carter was the worst thing that could happen to her.

Ha! She'd escaped that life but found more of the same, only worse. Mr. Carter was rich, and when he died, she would have been a very comfortable widow. He was far older than she. With luck, she'd have only a few years of wifely obligations to tolerate.

She looked at the man on the far side of the room and gulped. Compared to Mr. Carter her fiancé was young, healthy, and, from the state of his clothing, poor. At least her flesh didn't crawl when she looked at him, as it did with Mr. Carter. Instead, a heated shiver struck her.

Mr. Elliott idly rubbed his flat belly when it rumbled loudly. She flushed when hers answered the call. Hunger wasn't new to her and she'd often gone hungry on the train. However, three days of Sophie McLeod's wonderful food from the hotel dining room had reminded her belly that it could be filled.

With the poor state of this man's clothing, she'd be getting used to hunger again. She didn't mind if it brought her freedom. As a daughter, she was under her father's control. As a wife, she belonged to her husband. After weeks traveling on her own, she would not become a compliant wife like her mother. She would protect her children from everything, even their father if she had to. No child of hers would be beaten with a cane.

She heard the tinkle of spurs and scrape of boots on the wood floor when he shifted his feet. He watched her warily, as if she was dangerous. What would a man that big have to fear from her? She gulped. What had he done that required him to marry before he could enter Tanner's Ford? Sophie said to trust Sheriff Chambers, that he was a good, fair man.

She crossed her arms to hug herself. She had to marry a total stranger, dragged into the jail by the sheriff. Under these circumstances, how would he care anything about her or what she wanted from life?

His stomach rumbled again and he sighed. He turned more fully toward her and scratched his chest. Long legs clad in stained canvas trousers rose out of scuffed boots. An open buckskin coat revealed a shirt with missing buttons. His hands were huge, with long fingers. Dark hair dripped onto his shoulders. Like every other man, he wore a hat so her quick glance at his face only showed a strong nose above a thick moustache, all surrounded by heavy black stubble. He wore the usual faded gray bandana around his throat.

When he spoke, he'd croaked like a raven, his voice harsh and raw. She wouldn't judge him by that. Both her father and Mr. Carter spoke jovially with smiles and pleasant voices when they wished. Behind closed doors their true, violent nature emerged. The huge gun her fiancé had held in his right hand, cocked and steady, had stopped Charlie from hitting her.

All that didn't mean she wanted to marry him. Once again, men gave her no choice in her life. But it didn't matter. She'd marry this stranger rather than Big Joe. After all, she could always run away later.

"Evening, ma'am."

He spoke in the deep, rasping voice of a devil. She watched the brim of his hat drop as he looked from her tangled hair and dirty face to her ripped gown and equally filthy feet. Heat followed wherever he looked. A heat she was sure was indecent, though she'd never felt anything like it before. The fiancé her father chose had made her back away in disgust.

She curled her bare toes under her dress, both to hide them and to quell the hot shiver running through her. Her nipples budded as if a cold wind whistled past, yet a flush rose from her belly.

He was everything Mr. Carter was not. Young, handsome, dirty, and poor. If she was lucky, he might also be kind. However, luck was not a frequent visitor in her life.

His wide chest expanded with each deep breath as he watched her. She grasped her skirts with her fists to stop herself leaning toward him. Something pulled her to him, something strange and unnatural. She blinked for a long moment, then fought back as she had all her life. She'd had enough of men running her life. Too bad if the law said a husband owned his wife. With a strong first impression, half the battle was won. This one, she would win. She raised her nose and spoke like Mama would to one of her pretty sister's impertinent suitors.

"I am Miss Elizabeth Katherine James. I do not know you, sir."

The corner of his mouth twitched. He leaned back on his heels and rested his thumbs in his front pockets. Her eyes dropped at his movement. His tanned hands curled naturally, fingers framing taut pants. Pants that held what proper young virgins should not know about. She gulped, face heating. While locked up, she'd heard a few disgusting men boasting about what they wished to do to her with their unmentionable parts.

She raised her eyes to his shirt, but that wasn't safe either. Bleached from the sun and stained with who knows what, the fabric stretched over his chest. A jagged rip allowed dark curls to peek out. Missing buttons and frayed collar and cuffs proved the man needed a wife to keep him.

"Name's Trace Elliott, ma'am. You'll know me a whole lot better in the morning. After I make you my wife."

She choked at his quiet words and then coughed. A tornado of desire swirled up from her belly. When Mr. Carter ran his hands over her dress and tried to do more, she'd gagged and kneed him hard. Even though her father tried to beat her into marriage, she'd sworn she'd not let a man touch her again. But she'd never known a man could make her feel all fluttery.

"I have not agreed to the proposal put forward by Sheriff Chambers," she said, imitating her most prim teacher. "I do have options other than marriage." She looked down and dusted her dress from belly to hips as if brushing off a stray bit of fluff. It did nothing to the ground-in filth, unless dirt transferred to her hand from her brown traveling dress. She heard a sniff and the light clink of spurs as he shifted.

"Mistress or whore, ma'am?"

"I beg your pardon!" She straightened her back and gave him the full force of her most intimidating glare. After weeks of being ogled by odorous men, she'd perfected the look while quaking inside. He rubbed his finger under his nose where a bushy moustache obscured his lips.

"You're a woman. In Montana Territory, a female's got three choices. Wife, whore, or mistress." He looked at his hand as he counted them off. Thumb, pointing finger, middle finger. "If you throw out wife," he pulled his thumb back in, "that leaves two." He wiggled his two fingers at her. "Mistress or whore?"

She opened her mouth to speak but nothing came out. Her pounding heart seemed to twist, a sharp pain shooting from it to her head. She felt her lip curl.

"How dare you? I am a woman of good breeding!"

"Breeding don't matter out here 'less you're talking horses, cattle, or sheep."

"I would die first." She thrust the words out like spears, each one sharp and controlled.

"Your choice. Just stating the facts, ma'am." He pulled his mouth into a grimace and scratched the dark stubble on his right cheek with the fingers that had pointed out her fate.

"Mistress, now, that's a problem. The only single man in town able to pay for a fresh piece like you is Orville Rivers, the mayor." He shrugged and lifted his hands in a shrug. "He's the one said you had to get hitched tonight so I guess he's out. That leaves one choice." He held up his first finger and then pointed it toward her like a pistol. "Whore."

"No!"

"Miss Lily runs a right nice place," he continued calmly, as if she hadn't screamed at him. "I hear the whores at Baldy's Saloon do it fast and cheap. They spend most of the night on their back or their knees. Lily's gals, now, they only entertain a couple men a night. Costs more but you get a whole woman, not just a pussy." He touched his hat, not bothering to lift it. "Pardon, ma'am, but that's all it is to those drunken miners. The woman don't matter a'tall."

The walls pressed in on her as if she was already in her tomb. For a moment she heard nothing over the hoarse rasp of her violent breathing. Finally the deeper rasp of his voice penetrated her horror.

"Course, if we get hitched, you won't have to worry about that."

He stuck his thumbs in his gun belt and looked at her, eye to eye. She fought to keep from fainting, using his face as the only stable place in the spinning room.

He was right. She let out a shuddering breath. When she'd defiantly headed west it was with dreams of being a person in her own right. She would open a business of some kind, be a strong woman able to hold her own. She had no intention of being owned by a man.

Now it was time to face reality. She'd had her dreams, but they were now dust under her bare toes. Her reality would be marriage to this man. She'd live with him wherever he chose. From the look of him, it would be in a small cabin far from town, likely with a sod roof and dirt floor. No matter what he did to her, no one would know. Nor would they care, for she would belong to him, body and soul, until she died.

Sheriff Chambers had brought this man here to save her from

marrying a brute. She'd learned to trust the older man while she was in his jail. Sophie McLeod, the closest person to a friend she had, did as well. Elizabeth managed to calm her breathing but couldn't stop shaking. She clenched her hands behind her back. His eyes dropped to her chest.

"Bet you're pretty under all that dirt." She startled when he spoke, quiet and calm. She met his eyes. "Ma'am, I know I ain't much to look at. I wrecked my throat years ago and ended up with this croak so I don't talk much neither." He shook his head. "I said more tonight than in five or seven years altogether."

His dark eyes seemed to expand, enfolding her.

"Me and my brothers got a place on the Rocking E ranch west of town. Won't be much to a city gal like you, but it's home. We work long days and come home to bad cooking and a cold bed. It's not an easy life, but it's all I know. If we get hitched, I'll still work long days, but it'd be right nice to come home to good food and a warm bed."

She just stared at him. Her mind whirled so fast her ears buzzed like an angry swarm of bees. She knew about hard work. She'd cared for her grandparents and their hardscrabble farm. She'd worked dawn to dusk and then some, but she felt almost free. Only when her father decided to marry her off did he bring her back to the city, taking away her first taste of freedom.

She'd worked a farm once and she could do it again. But as a wife, it would be *her* home. She would decide what and how they ate. Not cantankerous old people who thought they still had a dozen servants rather than one too big, too strong, too opinionated granddaughter.

"You want me to marry you? This is what you get, ma'am." He held his hands wide, palms up.

Her fiancé was honest, both about himself and what he faced. She had to be as honest as to what she'd face, with or without him. How could marriage to this man be worse than her other options? When she didn't answer, he pursed his lips and nodded. He took a deep breath and then exhaled.

She looked at his broad chest and strong legs. With all the marks against him, he was still more of a man than any she'd seen in her life. Not pretty, rich, or well-mannered, he was tall enough that she felt almost normal. Not petite and sweet like her mother and sisters, but at least she didn't tower over him. Even better, he stood up to the bully of a deputy to protect her.

"Yes," she whispered.

His eyes narrowed. "Yes, what?" His hoarse rasp was worse, more of a grinding noise.

"Yes, I want you to marry me." She met his eyes. They stared at each other, neither breaking the glance. Heat rose from below her belly up her chest to her face. When it reached her cheeks she dropped her eyes to his boots, giving in to him.

But only for a moment. After one deep breath, she straightened, gritted her teeth, and stared into his face. One corner of his mouth lifted into a quick smile. His straightened and doffed his hat as if he strolled on a city's main street. No, he would never stroll unless he had a lady on his arm. This man would stride down the sidewalk, his boots loud on the wooden boards. With that smile and nod he went from ruffian to courtly, though unkempt, gentleman.

"But I..." She stopped. She concentrated for a moment before continuing. A wife had certain duties, horrid ones according to her mother. "Mr. Carter, the man my father wished me to marry, forced a kiss on me. It made me ill. Your touch may do the same."

"Did he hurt you?"

She shook her head at his growl. "I fought him off with my knee. He was most upset. So was Father." It had taken weeks for her bruises to fade after he broke his cane thrashing her. Never again.

"Good for you." He almost smiled at her. "Are you afraid of me hurting you? I've never raised a hand to hurt a woman."

A part of her heart melted at his gentle, encouraging words. She shook her head. Compared to the simmering violence shared by Big Joe and Charlie, she couldn't see him beating her.

"Then let me show you how a real man kisses his woman," he said. "You tell me to stop any time, and I will. But if you want more, I'll be glad to oblige."

His knowing wink sent chills through her body. He shrugged off his coat and hung it on a wall peg. She swallowed hard when he turned toward her. Eyes down, she watched his feet approach, the steps slow and steady. Eyes wide, nostrils flaring, he stalked her like an experienced bull after a heifer.

Never had a man looked at her like that. He didn't seem to care that she was too tall and loud. He knew nothing about her other than her refusal to be cowed.

He stopped with the scuffed toes of his boots only a few inches from her bare feet. She heard his rasping breath over the pounding of her heart. She inhaled a mixture of sweat, horse, tobacco, and something else. Something elusive, but tantalizing.

His hand rose, palm open, slow and sure. She watched it as she'd once seen a rabbit with a rattlesnake. The rabbit knew the end was near but could not move a muscle to escape.

"Shh," he whispered. "No one will ever hurt you again."

She heard no sign of his broken voice when he whispered. Her shoulders lowered as her tension retreated. His knuckle brushed the tip of her breast. She inhaled a gasp and lifted her eyes to him. He winked, lips twitching in amusement. Her nipples tightened in a way she'd never felt before. Her camisole pressed back against rising flesh, straining to meet his touch.

His fingers reached for her chin. He cupped it, holding her face still. His dark eyes watched her as if learning more about her than anyone, including herself, would ever know.

"I'm going to kiss you now."

She gulped again and inhaled. He brushed chapped lips against hers, his moustache lightly scraping her skin. A shiver ran outward from his touch. A deep throbbing followed, reaching her neck, bosom, belly, and even lower. She pressed her thighs together, not knowing why but trying to ease the needy feeling.

He nibbled on her bottom lip with gentle teeth. He slid his tongue along the crease between her lips. She opened to his kiss, wondering at how good it felt, how right. She pressed her palms against his hard chest. It wasn't enough. She slipped her arms around him, stepping close so her breasts pressed against him. He moaned and his tongue entered her, unleashing a firestorm of need. She clung to him, rising on her toes to capture more of him, demanding more.

He was the one who finally pulled back, leaving both of them gasping. Her blood sang through her veins, flashing like white lightning from point to point. He shuddered and pressed her head against his chest. He wrapped his arms around her.

If he hadn't, she would have sunk to the floor, boneless.

Never had she felt so safe. She reveled in his embrace for a moment and then rested her palms against his chest.

His strength made her want to give up all her worries, breaching the tall walls she'd built to protect herself from shame and humiliation. If she let him in, she would lose everything that had kept her going when no one cared about her. She would be far too vulnerable.

No. Giving in to a husband was not how to begin a marriage. Especially if one touch from the man made her crave him even more. She pushed on his chest. After a moment, he released her. He stepped back, frowning and breathing hard. She shook out her skirts and pressed her hair off her forehead with both palms as she thought. How to proceed to gain some control? All her life she'd been accused of speaking too forcefully. For once, it would be to her benefit.

"If I must marry, I want a husband who sees me as a partner, not a beast of burden. One who won't beat me or our children." She met his eyes with a glare. "A *real* man doesn't need to use his fists."

"You don't have a choice in this." She inhaled to rail at him but stopped when he held up his flat palm. "Neither do I. But Elliotts don't hold with beating women, children, or beasts. My ma was a strong woman and demanded respect. I need a wife who's tough enough to do what's needed. It's a hard life for everyone with more than enough work to keep a body going from before morning light to after dark. Does that make me man enough for you?"

He looked at her, calm and sure. Her heart pounded so hard she felt faint. He was a man all right, but nothing like those she knew.

"I, uh, I'm not sure. You could say anything, and I'd not know if you meant it. The only men I know well are from back East. I've never even seen my father or brother without a coat, much less felt their arms around me. I don't know how to judge you, as a man or a husband."

She licked her lips as he stared down at her. She hadn't known a man could heat a woman with only his eyes. She fought to keep still, to not beg for his touch once again. Like Adam and Eve, she'd tasted the forbidden fruit and learned what modest women must never crave. She had knowledge of the wonder of physical desire and was changed forever. Would the touch of his hand on her bare skin do even more to set her afire? This was what made women run off with unsuitable men.

"Well, I ain't no Eastern dude afraid to take off his coat and roll up his shirt sleeves to work." He glanced toward the door, then back to her. She saw a hint of a devilish grin. "How about I show you what you're getting. Do you want to see what's under my shirt, Beth?"

Beth.

He branded her with that one word, whispered with desire. She'd come to Tanner's Ford as Elizabeth Katherine James. It was a proper name for the daughter of an important man. That life was gone. Soon, she'd be Mrs. Trace Elliott, his Beth.

Before she said her vows to this stranger, she would see the flesh she'd clung to. After spending three days and two nights in jail her virtue was long gone. She could flout society's rules without falling further in disgrace. If the man who would be her husband wanted to show off his muscles, she would not deny him. She nodded.

He flashed a smile, stepped away and tossed his hat onto the sheriff's desk. Dark hair, pressed tight against his big head from his hat, curled to his shoulders. Watching her closely, he took his dusty bandana from around his neck. A raised white scar ran around his neck from collar to chin, as if he'd been hanged or dragged with a rope. That's what happened with horse thieves or murderers. Had he escaped a noose?

He slowly unbuttoned his worn shirt. Arm and chest muscles shifted as he moved. He took it off and tossed it to the desk. Tiny imitations of her own nipples peeked out from his chest hair. His arms certainly looked strong enough to work all day. A few scars here and there showed he'd not spent his time as a clerk in an office. The dark curls on his chest looked soft. A matching line led down to…a bulge.

She gasped when he stepped close and took her waist in both large hands. Heat flared, a heat that shot down to her private place. She automatically set her hands on his thick forearms for balance. He raised her off the ground until they were eye to eye, her toes dangling. He lifted her as if she was petite, like her pretty, popular younger sisters.

"You'll live on the Rocking E with me and two of my brothers. Me, Jack, and Simon will take care of you. We'll do what a man does for his wife."

Share a small cabin with *three* men? But it was still better than her other choices. He waited for her answering nod. Both of them panting, he held her to his chest so her body dragged against his. Under her dirty dress her hard nipples, protruding from swollen breasts, scraped against his naked chest. When she touched down, the gritty wood floor felt cool against the soles of her feet. He leaned close. His naked chest waited mere inches from her nose. Raw strength and power oozed from every pore. He held himself as if he needed no gun to prove he was a man. Secure in himself, he didn't depend on money, clothing, or society to know who he was.

"In return, you'll take care of us."

He rubbed his hard stomach against her chest, rasping her nipples through the fabric. A bolt of desire shot between her legs. This was what she'd been warned about, the wicked attraction a decent woman had to fight. They said only low women allowed a man's touch without shuddering in revulsion.

She shuddered, but in desire.

He moved her matted hair behind her shoulders with long fingers. He bent and nuzzled her neck. She quivered even more when he brought his lips to her ear.

"You'll do everything a wife does for her husband," he whispered. "Everything." He gently bit the lobe of her ear. A shaft of white-hot desire set her on fire. "In my bed and anywhere else I want you."

Without the rasping croak, his sultry whisper shivered down her spine like ice water. The warm air from his breath teased her neck for a moment. He panted as hard as she. He lifted his lips and nibbled his way to her jaw. Her body arched toward him before she knew it, hard nipples scraping against his naked chest. Only a few thin layers of fabric separated them. He wrapped his arms around her and nipped her earlobe. She grabbed him to hold herself up as her knees buckled.

"That's right, darlin'. Hold me tight."

She clung to him, reveling in the caring touch of another. She couldn't remember the comfort of a warm body holding her close. Had never felt the desire that this man brought into her world. How had she lived and not known this delight existed?

Starved for affection, knowing she would soon marry him and could enjoy this again, she gave in to his touch.

She moaned when his hand slid up her ribcage. She inhaled a hiss when he weighed her breast. His thumb pressed her nipple, shooting sparks through her greedy body. He pinched lightly and fire exploded as if he branded her.

When he groaned and stepped back, she found the energy to

inhale. Barely. He lifted her chin with his knuckle. She blinked up at him, frozen in place.

"I'm a big man, as are my brothers," he whispered. "But you're a passionate woman with enough flesh to hold on to."

He grasped her bottom with both hands and pulled her tight against him. His fingers spread her cheeks apart in a most unsettling manner. His hard manhood pressed against her belly. He groaned, low and hungry.

She looked up at the sound, biting her lip. Dark eyes bored into hers. He leaned down, and she knew he was going to kiss her again. She'd slapped her fiancé's face when he tried, bringing on another beating from her father. But this felt so different.

She opened her mouth. The first light touch of his lips tantalized her. He slid his tongue between her top lip and teeth. Her legs gave way, and he pulled her close with a heated promise.

She nestled closer to his warm chest, feeling his heartbeat pound through her thin dress. His strong arms held her, protecting rather than confining. She relaxed into his possessive embrace, aroused and safe in his arms. She could let him do these wonderful things to her body without relinquishing control in their home.

He pulled his mouth away, resting his forehead against hers. She blinked, the dim light bright on her eyes. Her skin rose in gooseflesh, cold without his heat.

"Am I man enough for you, Beth?" She stared at him, unable to think, much less talk for a moment. She nodded. He inhaled a deep breath. When he let it out the tension seemed to release as well. He sniffed her hair.

"You smell nice," he murmured.

She snorted at his words, breaking the mesmerizing spell. "I smell like I've lived in a privy for weeks."

"Nothing a bath won't cure." He took her hand and towed her toward the corner desk and the kerosene lamp providing light. He hooked the chair with one foot and sat, then pulled her onto his lap. It put her breasts about the height of his mouth.

"Tell me about yourself," he said. He looked her in the eye, no longer laughing, as if he actually cared what her reply might be. She went along, just in case.

"I was born in Philadelphia twenty-one years ago."

He nodded for her to continue, still watching her. She said the most outrageous thing she could think of.

"I have an education, my brain works well, and I enjoy using it. I like to know what is happening around me, and I expect to have my opinions listened to." She set her teeth and waited for the explosion. He merely lifted an eyebrow at her silence. "I will not tolerate excessive use of spirits nor abuse of any kind."

He grasped her upper thigh, his hand covering the whole of the portion resting on his leg, and grinned at her. She'd hidden her reactions for weeks as men leered at her, expecting her to jump into their arms merely because she rode the Bride Train. Now that she was safe, her anger rose from where she'd hidden it deep inside.

"Do you think my demands laughable?"

She struggled to get off his lap, suddenly furious. He put his arms around her so she could not escape and laughed, a rough cawing noise that grated her ears. Her father used to laugh at her pitiful efforts to speak her mind. He enjoyed humiliating his inferiors, especially his wife and children. She fought to escape.

"Shh, Beth, I'm not laughing at you," he growled. "It's just that you sound like Ma. She taught all seven of us to read, write, do sums and debate. I remember Pa getting Ma all riled up by debating the opposite of whatever she said. Though he wasn't yet twelve when they died, Ben says getting a word in between Ma and Pa was good practice for being a lawyer."

His words finally seeped through her anger. It took a few minutes before she realized he was not trying to keep her from escaping. Rather, he supported her so she did not fall to the floor in her mad rush for freedom. She shuddered and let him hold her temple against him. His heart pounded as madly as hers.

"Beth, I said I don't beat women, children, or animals. A mule can't help being a mule anymore than a woman can help being who she is. Or a man," he continued when she poked him in the chest with her fingernail. He caught her fist and kissed it, slowly and sensuously, daring her with his eyes to retaliate when he released her.

He leaned forward and tilted his head, waiting. Determined to prove her lack of fear, she met him halfway, demanding rather than merely accepting. He pulled her close and kissed her, lightly scraping his rough whiskers on her chin. She ran her fingers through his hair, holding him tight to her.

"Whoa!" A deep, laughing voice came from the far door. "The bedding's supposed to happen after the preacher speaks, not before." Sheriff Chambers stepped into the jail, followed by the hotel owner, Sophie McLeod.

Beth leaped back as if she'd touched a hot stove. Luckily, Trace was more aware. He caught her before she fell off his lap. He pulled her tight to him, giving her strength to face the preacher and witnesses following the sheriff. She was allowed to touch him as this man would soon be her husband.

"Looks like you found yourself a husband just in time," said Sophie with a chuckle. They'd chatted when she brought meals to Beth at the jail. Sophie set her fists on her hips and grinned widely at the two of them. "I never thought the day would come when Trace Elliott would find himself a wife."

"He didn't," said the sheriff. "I found her for him. And if we don't get this done afore certain parties arrive, the preacher will be holding a funeral instead of a wedding."

He pointed to where he wanted Trace and Beth to stand. Trace helped an unsteady Beth to her feet.

A shabby man dressed in black shuffled up to them. He lifted bleary red eyes, nodded at the bride and groom, and then opened his dusty book.

"The boys're holding a place for me at the poker table, so's lets get this over with," ordered the preacher. "Dearly beloved, we are gathered here to unite these two in holy matrimony." He looked around the room. "No one with a reason to complain here. Trace Elliott do you take this gal—" He barely raised his head to see her. "What's your name, missy?"

"Elizabeth Katherine James."

He blinked at her, then turned. "Trace Elliott, you take this gal for yer wife? You'll bed her and breed her and care for her best you can all yer days so help you God?"

"Yessir."

"And you, woman. You promise to take this man into your bed, care for him, his family, and whatever young'uns come along for the rest of your life so help you God?"

"Um, yes, I do."

"Is there a ring?"

Trace shook his head.

"Nope? Well, then hold hands."

Trace held his open palm to her. She placed her hand on his and he engulfed it with the other. The preacher put his hands on top and silently prayed for a moment. He flashed a clear look at Beth. It seared her soul and proved that God was in the room no matter that the words weren't right and the preacher reeked of whiskey and tobacco. The room seemed less bright when he removed his hands from theirs.

"Yer now man and wife in God's eyes and no man can say nay once the beddin's done." He closed his book and then turned to Trace. "Yer ma and pa are lookin' down on ye, boy. You be as good a man as yer pa and this gal will do right fine." He sniffed and rubbed his nose with the back of his hand. "Sheriff says ye'll put gold in the poor box for this." Trace nodded. "Then what's holdin' yah back, boy? Kiss yer bride and get her to bed afore Big Joe hears of it!"

Trace pulled her tight against him. At first he nibbled, but soon he explored her mouth with his tongue as his hands roved her body. Only the two of them existed until Trace suddenly pulled away, gasping.

"Any rooms at that hotel of yours, Mrs. McLeod?" said Frank Chambers. "These two need one about now."

Sophie laughed. "I sent Elspeth to prepare the best room and get a hot bath ready for the new Mrs. Elliott. You," she said, pointing a finger at Trace, "will find facilities elsewhere." She flapped her hands to separate the two of them. "Don't bother visiting until you're clean and shaved." She turned to Beth. "Mrs. Elliott, would you like a hot bath? I have a deep tub that would fit you."

The new Mrs. Trace Elliott, dazed from more than the kiss, nodded. She focused on the bath, ignoring what would come after. Like her sisters, as a young girl she'd imagined her wedding day as being sunny and bright. Wearing a pretty white dress, she'd stand in the church beside a rich, handsome man in a suit. Though her dreams faded by her late teens, never had she considered she'd be part of a forced union between a bedraggled slattern and dusty cowboy.

Trace placed his hand on her arm, stopping her from turning away.

"I know I'm not the husband you wanted and this isn't the wedding you dreamed of." He looked around the drab, dingy jail and shook his head. "A woman should feel good at her wedding."

"Where'd you learn about women?" The sheriff snorted. "Three brothers living out there alone for how many years?"

"Before she died, Ma taught me how to treat a lady. My wife is a lady and deserves to be treated like one. This may be a rough start, but I'll make it up her. She'll have no complaints."

Beth looked up at her new husband. Body trembling, she fought sudden tears. She promised herself long ago to never let it show when she was afraid, but kindness was something she'd rarely experienced. She blinked rapidly, turning her head away to hide. He took her face in his hands and gently forced her to look up at him.

"Shh. You're my wife now. I'll kill any man who tries to hurt you."

His first words were tender. He likely thought the last ones were also. Was he saying he would defend his property or that he wouldn't let anyone hurt her because he cared for her?

No, he didn't care for her as a person. He'd only met her and knew nothing other than she was a means to an end. It didn't matter. She was no longer alone, fighting to hold her head up when those who should love her, hurled abuse. Though she fought to hold them back, tears spilled down her cheeks. She wiped them away with the back of her dirty hand.

"Where's my strong woman? The one who knocked Charlie down with one punch?" He gently kissed her forehead. "A hot bath, food, and clean clothes will make you feel better. But you'll have to wait a while to sleep." His wink brought new heat to her face.

He escorted her to the door, then pressed her arm to wait. She took the moment to pull herself together. She almost lost composure again when he slipped his soft buckskin coat over her shoulders to keep her warm and protect her modesty. She gasped when he swept her into his arms and carried her out the door.

"I'll not have my wife walk in the street in bare feet." He carried her across the muddy, manure-strewn street and set her down carefully on the boardwalk in front of the hotel. "The faster you get clean the sooner I get to kiss what's under all that dirt," he whispered in her ear. He slid his hands between her dress and his coat, grasped her bottom, and pulled her close. Evidence of his desire blazed across her belly.

"Don't take too long, wife. I want to make you mine."

Chapter Three

Trace scraped his cheek with a straight razor borrowed from Miss Lily. He had to tilt his head to avoid the mirror's cracks and black pits. He nicked himself again and swore as he rinsed the blade in the bowl of warm water. He'd stared down catamounts, vicious killers, and rattlesnakes. Yet a city woman like Beth scared the hell out of him.

She was no pretty-but-weak flower like Gillis MacDougal's wife, Prudence. None of them could believe it when Gillis returned from his trip East with a wife dressed in silk ruffles and satin bows. They'd shrugged and gone on with their lives until the dang sheriff realized Gillis was no longer joining them in town on a Saturday night to whoop it up and take the miners down a few pegs. Because Gillis didn't join them anymore, Frank Chambers got it in his fool head that a married man caused less trouble.

The last time all three Elliotts hit town they'd had a wonderful time. Just before Christmas they'd worked their way through a half-dozen drunken miners. They were winning until Hugh Jennet, the sanctimonious banker, complained to the sheriff about the noise. Trace, Simon, and Jack were hauled off to jail. Frank tossed the miners out of town.

The next morning, he'd done the same to Trace and his brothers, decreeing that no Elliott was allowed back until one of them married. Just because Gillis MacDougal stopped being fun once he married, didn't mean that a rip-snorting Elliott man would. Bets were on Jack to marry, if any of them. The boy could even sweet-talk Miss Lily's gals into sharing their bed on a quiet night.

No one would believe he'd be the one that got caught. And by such a woman!

His Beth was nothing like Gillis's sickly wife. Put Prudence in a jail cell with the town's ruffians ogling her and she'd faint dead away. She'd start in the coughing again, and in three days they'd be calling the undertaker.

Unlike his best friend's wife, Beth had gumption, along with a body that would soon be his.

Trace swelled, remembering the flesh he'd held in the jail before their brief wedding. She'd responded to him like a wildcat in heat. From her shocked reaction to her response, she'd never known pleasure. All he wanted from a wife was passion, respect, and friendship. Awakening that passion was his job for tonight.

A tough job, but he was man enough for it.

He wiped his face off and stared at the fractured image. He was exactly as he looked. A tough, hard-working cowboy fighting to make a home for himself and his brothers. Since Pa died, he'd taken orders from no one and wasn't about to start now. Especially from a woman. She could be feisty all she liked, but there was only one ramrod on a ranch, and he was it for the Rocking E.

The doorknob rattled. He'd turned and palmed his gun by the time the door opened. The petite woman raised a plucked eyebrow at his drawn weapon. "That's not what most husbands would point at a woman after their wedding," she said. She winked when he flushed.

"They wouldn't be bathing in your private quarters either." He stuck his gun back in its holster. "Thanks for lending me a place to wash up, Lily."

"I'm the closest thing to an aunt you have north of Texas. I couldn't do less for my favorite nephew." She tilted her perfectly made up face up at him. "You can't go to your bride with ragged hair hanging down your back." She walked to stand beside him, her forehead barely reaching his nipples though she wore heels. "It's a wife's job to trim her man's hair, but I'd like to tidy you up a bit before she sees you up close and personal."

When he hesitated she snapped her fingers and pointed at a backless chair. He shrugged and sat down. She wrapped his damp towel around his shoulders and picked up her scissors.

"Tilt your head. I hear you got yourself a wife to suit you. Frank and his missus like her and so does Sophie. She visited Patsy Tanner at the mercantile a fair bit and made some high fashion dress sketches, which Patsy showed me. To top it off, since Eudora and Hugh Jennet and Mayor Rivers don't like her, she's gold in my books." Lily began snipping so his hair would just touch his collar. "Tell me about her."

"Don't know much about her other than she's got spirit," said Trace. "She's been beaten, but it didn't stop her fighting back. Though she looked scared spitless, she stood up to Charlie. She held her fists high, ready to plow him." His lip twitched in memory. "She got him good in the jaw, he tripped, and he went down hard on his ass."

"Hmm, that's not the story Charlie's telling at Baldy's. How well does she fit you?"

"Won't know that until I take her to bed," he replied with a wink. She slapped the side of his head in mock fierceness.

"You've at least kissed her?" She lifted the scissors from his ear when he agreed. "Well, how did she feel in your arms?"

Trace thought back. His arms had wrapped around her like they were made to be there. When she hugged him back, he felt a deep contentment that he'd forgotten existed.

"She fit."

Lily, madam of Tanner's Ford's house of ill-repute, smiled like sunshine. "You boys deserve a good woman." She finished her work and rolled up the towel. She replaced her scissors and tidied up. Trace watched her move around the room.

Fate had steered him into town tonight, just as it had the night he saved Lily from three attackers. Knowing the consequences, he'd do both again. Beth needed a strong man to care for her, one she could trust. From what she said, she had good reason not to trust men. It might take some time for her to learn that Elliotts kept their word. No lies, no evasions. When he said something, it was true. Even if she didn't like it.

"I hear the preacher made it quick. Did he skip anything important?"

"I promised to bed, breed, and care for Beth the best I can. He said nothing about love and honor." Lily waited. He waggled his head and sighed. "My wife did not promise to obey me."

Lily laughed. "Wonderful! She won't have it on her conscience when she does what she needs to. With the three of you in one house, she'll be a busy woman, day and night." She walked over to Trace on tiny feet and crooked her finger. He bent over so she could place a chaste kiss on his cheek. "What will you do to encourage her to take on all three of you?"

"I'll show her what Trixie and Felicity taught me all those years ago." He returned the kiss, planting it gently on her forehead.

"Damn you, Trace Elliott! If you were thirty years older, I might have hauled you to the altar long ago."

"Granny, Gran, or Grandma?" He tossed off the question as if it was a joke, but her reaction quickly sobered him.

She stopped, one hand pressed to her heart. "You'd let me see your children?"

He pulled her close, her cheek resting against his bare chest. "I want my children to have a grandmother."

"But I'm a whore," she said. "Your wife might not want me near her children."

"Dammit, Lily. That job might have kept your body alive for a while, but that's not who you are." Her hot tears trailed their way down his belly, yet she made no sound. "Yes, you run a whorehouse. But your girls are here because they want to be. Any of them could marry and be gone, but you treat them right, pay them well, and everyone gets what they want. I'd rather have my sister working here than married to a hard case like Joe Sheldrake."

"Your father wouldn't want to hear you say that about Jessamine."

"Pa chose to die beside Ma rather than fight to live and care for seven children who needed him. I don't give a damn about him!"

The silence ran loud for a minute.

"Beth will do what's right. She raised her nose like Mrs. Emslow when Frank introduced us, but that changed fast when I kissed her. A few weeks with me and the boys and she'll come around." He chuckled and gave Lily a squeeze. "I bet she can be just as cantankerous as a certain bawdy lady, so you two should get along fine. Maybe Rosa could teach her how to cook.

"You're a good man, Trace Elliott. I'll send word that Beth has my protection. Any man who treats her without respect won't set foot in my parlor again. That should cut down the number of unwanted visitors stopping by."

"Joe Sheldrake's the only one likely to cause trouble. He had plans for Beth. He'll take this as a threat, especially as we've never seen eye to eye."

"He's not smart enough to do much on his own, but I've heard rumors he's the link between that vigilante gang and someone here in Tanner's Ford."

"You tell that to Frank?"

"Of course. I've always thought he had something to do with that scar around your throat. He's too much of a coward to face you head on. He'll hire men to do his dirty work, so tell Beth to be wary of strangers."

"Always." Trace kissed Lily's forehead, careful not to disturb her neatly curled hair. "You take care of yourself, Grannie."

"Grandchildren of my own." Lily moved far enough back to look up at him. She blinked her eyes but a few tears overflowed. "I never cry," she murmured, more to herself. She dabbed at her eyes with the lace-trimmed handkerchief she pulled from her sleeve. "My face must be ruined." He let her go when she stepped back. "I'd better get back downstairs. I've got a business to run." She settled herself back into her official persona and walked toward the door. She opened it and then turned to face him. "I prefer Gram," she said and closed the door behind her.

Trace stared after her for a moment. Only now did he realize how much she meant to him. He didn't remember much during the time she kept him from dying, other than pain. Doc said it was touch and go for a while, but he couldn't die on his siblings like his parents had. Once he healed enough to ride, he returned to the Rocking E. For years he was too busy raising his younger brothers and running the ranch to think of a family.

No decent woman would want him, so he'd pushed almost everyone away. A few times a year, his need for comfort got too strong, and he visited one of Lily's girls for a night. The rest of the time he took out his frustration and anger in work and fist fights against the damned land-raping miners. Only now, allowing himself to believe his dream might come true, did he let memories drift in.

He drew on his shirt and buttoned it. Enough of the past, tonight was all about his future. Their future. With Beth's cooperation, there'd be children to pass the Elliott legacy on to. He wanted lots. If only Ranger, Ben, and Patrick would return from Texas. Get at least one of them married and in a few generations there'd be more damn Elliotts around Tanner's Ford than a body could shake a stick at.

First step was to bed his bride. Maybe he'd make Jack and Simon sleep in the barn until he gentled her. He'd get her used to enjoying her body with him. He'd teach her how to accept, and give, pleasure in every way. From the way she'd reacted to his touch, the lady had passion to spare. That was a good thing. One brother couldn't bring a wife home and have the others go without.

By fall they'd be settled in a new routine. He stretched, a slow grin of satisfaction settling in. He'd wake up to decent coffee, porridge, ham, and gravy with hot biscuits and jam. She'd bring their dinner to them at the nooning. When they came home tired and hungry at night, she'd fill their bellies.

And, when the evening chores were done, they'd fill her with their heat.

* * * *

"That's one big man you married, girl."

Beth kept quiet as Sophie poured a bucket of rinse water over her clean hair. Sophie's wedding present was a room, meals, and, best of all, a hot soak in the big copper tub. It reminded Beth of what pleasures life could bring.

"Lily's girls say the Elliott men are big all over. They're gentleman, though they do love a rip-roaring fight." Finished with the water, Sophie rubbed Beth's hair with a towel. She leaned close. "I hear Trace doesn't visit as often as they'd like. Rosa the cook told me the gals say he's a very good lover." She bent closer to Beth's ear. "They say he's got all sorts of wicked ideas. I even heard that once or twice the three brothers shared a girl. Rosa said they plumb tired her out, but she had a big smile on her face for days."

"Please!" Beth sat up, stopping Sophie. "I don't want to hear that on my wedding night. Or *any* night."

"Couldn't tell that from the way you and Trace looked when we walked into the jail." She held out a towel when Beth sputtered. "How about this? Big Joe's locked up."

"Thank goodness." Beth took the offered towel, eager to distance herself from her experienced friend's words. "I was worried he might try to attack us during our wedding night. I wouldn't have been able to sleep if he was free."

"I heard it took eight men to drag Joe from Baldy's Saloon and stuff him in that jail cell. I'm surprised Trace missed the opportunity for a good fight." She shrugged. "I wouldn't be surprised if Joe was one of those who roped and dragged Trace through town. No," she said, forestalling Beth's questions. "You'll have to ask him about it."

Beth was quiet while she settled in front of the fire. Sophie began combing out the worst knots in Beth's hair. The bowl of thick pea and bacon soup she'd eaten before her bath had settled her stomach. While she soaked away weeks of dirt, she'd had a chance to think.

By marrying an unkempt stranger, she'd been spared humiliation, pain, and perhaps death. She owed her life to Trace. But she'd not come all this way to have a man control her. Thanks to the absent-minded preacher, she'd not promised to obey her husband. Had Trace noticed? Would what they had promised matter to him, or would he do what he liked anyway? No matter. She chose poor ranch hand Trace Elliott over both a rich Philadelphia banker and a Western brute. She would make an effort to be a good wife.

"Do you know anything about my husband's family?"

Now that the worst of the knots were out, Sophie's rhythmic movements soothed Beth. Enjoying the unusual caring touch, Beth let Sophie take her time to answer.

"I don't tell stories or gossip. I can say the Elliotts arrived with the MacDougal family even before John and Patsy Tanner stopped their loaded wagon and created Tanner's Ford. Trace was a small boy when he arrived, and I don't think he's been past Bannack City since." Sophie paused. She tapped the comb against her cheek. "No, I think he went all the way to Virginia City once. Finan MacDougal took a wagonload of boys with him for some reason. The Elliott ranch is called the Rocking E. It's on the northeast side of the valley to the west of town. The MacDougals have the M-D Connected on the southwest side of the valley."

"Wait," said Beth. She pushed hair off her face to see Sophie. "My husband said he worked on the Rocking E ranch. I thought he was a hired hand."

"Trace Elliott, a hired hand?" Sophie laughed. "I expect you also thought he has nothing but a plugged nickel to his name." Beth nodded. Sophie pointed the comb at her. "You are one lucky woman. Not only is your husband a good man, his family owns some of the best ranch land around. They might not have cash money, but you'll never go hungry." She barked a laugh. "Unless those boys clean out the larder now that they've got a woman cooking for them. You'd better stock up before you leave town. After a long, hard winter, those boys will have their bellies stuck to their backbones if Simon or Jack's been cooking. Can you cook or are you one of those useless Eastern city women?"

Beth glared. "I am not useless. I cared for my grandparents' farm the last couple of years. All but the oldest servants were dead or gone. I can cook, put up food, sew—"

"Whoa!" Sophie backed away as Beth's voice rose. "That's good. Those Elliott boys need a strong woman to stand up to them. If I were you, I'd pray to whoever sent Trace into town tonight. Bend your head and let me finish your hair."

Beth let the moment pass until they both calmed. "How did Trace get that scar around his neck?"

"He didn't escape hanging as a horse thief, if that's what you're thinking." Beth's cheeks flamed. "He saved a woman when he was barely eighteen. They came after him and dragged him behind a horse with a rope around his neck."

"How did he survive?"

"He's an Elliott," said Sophie. "Too damn stubborn to give up. Tilt your head."

Beth did as she was told. Every moment brought her closer to the time her husband would demand his marital rights. One afternoon her mother explained wifely duties to Beth and her sisters. She said the husband does painful, disgusting things to his wife's body. He does this as often as he chooses until she produces two sons. Then he returns to his mistress.

Beth had been horrified. Luckily, her friend Florence Peabody's older sister married shortly after. She'd whispered to both girls that marital relations could be enjoyable with the right man. When Beth asked how one would know the right one, she was told her body would tingle when he touched her.

Trace made her tingle, even while still across the room. And when he kissed her…

"You have beautiful hair," said Sophie as she finished. "And look what Miss Lily sent over for you." At Beth's horrified gasp, Sophie shook her head. "It's a nightgown fit for a bride, Beth, not anything disrespectful. And please don't judge what you don't know. Trace was only sixteen when his parents died from a spring fever. Lily became like an aunt to the eldest three boys. The MacDougals took in the others."

Sophie lifted the filmy white nightgown from the bed. Though warm from the fire, Beth shivered as the delicate fabric slid over her naked flesh. It covered her skin from neck to wrist to toes but hid nothing. She blushed when Sophie winked.

"Miss Lily has an eye for what a man wants to see." Sophie sighed. "Maybe one day she'll find something like that for my wedding night."

A sharp rap on the door made her jump. The handle rattled but Sophie had bolted the door.

"Where's my bride?" The growl was unmistakable.

"Keep your pants on," replied Sophie. "Mrs. Elliott needs time to get ready for her first night with you. You'll have the rest of your lives together so have patience."

"I want to start that life now!" Though the deep voice demanded action, neither woman jumped to obey.

"She'll be ready when she's ready. Did you get a wedding ring or a bride present yet?"

"Wedding ring's at home." The floor creaked as he shifted his feet. "My wife can pick a present from the mercantile in the morning."

A thrill went through Beth at the thought of a present. Would he allow her to get material for a new dress? Not anything fancy, but she'd only brought two, both ugly. She wanted to burn the one she'd worn in jail along with the humiliating memories. The sheriff kindly returned her boots, well shined, with a pair of stockings from his wife.

"Beth?" This time his voice crooned, making her shiver and not in fear. "Make that tomorrow *afternoon* at the mercantile. You'll stay in my bed until then."

The low chuckle following his footsteps down the hallway raised Beth's nipples as her breasts swelled in anticipation, though she wasn't sure of what. She bit her lip, staring at the door.

"Never thought Trace Elliott would find a woman who wasn't afraid of him." Grinning, Sophie shook her head and sighed. "Most girls take one look at his huge body, piercing eyes, and broken voice and run to their mamas. But you want the man."

Beth didn't deny it. "Why would anyone be afraid of him?"

"Why?" Sophie backed away to look up at Beth's reflection. "Even with your size, if that man slapped you with his big hand, you'd fly across the room and smash into a wall. And that voice, like the croaking of a raven just waiting for someone to die so it can peck out your eyes." Sophie smiled, though her words made Trace sound like a monster worse than Big Joe.

"Trace told me Elliotts never hit a woman, child, or animal. Is that true?"

Beth stared in the mirror and waited for her new friend to answer. Sophie, standing behind, lifted Beth's hair and set it to flow down her back.

"That man and his brothers love a knock-down, street brawling fight, especially against miners. They were banned from town because they always won. But they don't get mean drunk, and they've never hit anyone who didn't deserve it." She poked Beth in the back to make her stand straight. "You'd better tell him you need to keep this gown in one piece. Otherwise he'll rip it open to get at you. Mind, you're likely the first present he's unwrapped in years. Not that this gown hides a dang thing."

Beth blushed at her friend's wicked smile. She left her hair loose, ripples of gold falling to her bottom. She didn't have to pinch her cheeks for color as, whenever she thought of what might come later, her face flamed.

Sophie opened the door and leaned her head out. "You ready down there, Mr. Elliott?"

"Hell, yeah!"

Beth swallowed hard at the deep laughter floating up at Trace's reply. This was it. She'd run from the only home she knew to escape a horrid marriage and ended up in jail.

Jail, marriage, what was the difference? She was now Trace's property. Her mother said a woman's last decision in life was her promise to God saying, "I do." Every decision after that belonged to her husband. Not as far as Elizabeth Katherine James Elliott was concerned. Getting married didn't turn her brain to mush or diminish her desire for fulfillment. It did, however, make parts of her quiver that she hadn't known existed.

"This'll help keep your hands from trembling," said Sophie, handing her a small posy. A damp cloth wrapped around their stems kept them from wilting. Beth accepted the sweet violets. She hesitantly sniffed but couldn't catch their scent.

"Thank you so much. They're beautiful! But how did you have time to pick them?"

"Your husband brought them for you. He said a woman should have flowers on her wedding day."

Beth blinked rapidly as her posy, now even more precious, blurred. Sophie shook her head and winked. "You've married into a family of good men. And I think you're cussed enough to take them on." She kissed Beth's cheek.

"Thank you. For everything," Beth whispered.

"You are most welcome. Now smile for your man. He'll make a good husband if you let him lead the way."

Head high, clutching her flowers, Beth waited for her husband.

Chapter Four

Trace, hearing Sophie's call, clenched his fists tight and held still. Anything to stop from rushing up the stairs like a boy eager for his first woman. While the ceremony at the jail joined Beth to him in law, it could still be annulled. Once he joined with her flesh to complete the bond, she'd be his forever. Every soft, precious, cantankerous inch of her.

He could touch her whenever he wanted, do anything he chose to her and not even God would have the right to say no. He'd never force Beth, but he would seduce and encourage her into doing things she'd never known existed. Starting now.

Sophie gave a saucy wink as she passed him on the stairs. Damn, he was hard, but Beth was a virgin. He'd have to make her first time so good she'd want more. Much more.

He counted the slow steps, wincing as his thighs brushed against his groin with every movement. He knocked quietly before opening the door. She had her back to him. The soft glow of a lamp in the window lit the spun gold hair cascading over her shoulders. It covered everything but her rounded bottom and long legs. He longed to thrust into the dark cleft between her thighs. Then he'd bend her forward and slide into her wet heat. She slowly turned to face him, steps hesitant and jerky. It provided a sideways silhouette that made him groan in appreciation.

"Thank you for the flowers," she said, eyes flickering around the room. "They're beautiful. I've never been given flowers before."

She held them between full breasts. On either side, rosy tips pointed at him like bullets. Her lip quivered, and he realized she was waiting for him to say something. His tongue felt glued to the top of his mouth. He swallowed hard and finally inhaled.

"You're even more beautiful than I thought, Mrs. Elliott," he croaked.

Her eyes glistened and she blinked hard. Did she cry at the thought of marrying him? Then she hardened her jaw and straightened her back. She tossed her hair like a filly eager to play.

"You clean up pretty well yourself, Mr. Elliott."

When he claimed her full lips in the jail after their vows, he almost came on the spot. She had gazed up at him with a glassy look when he released her. Then she smiled with, he hoped, eagerness for more. He wasn't a church-going man, but he thanked God he landed in town tonight.

And now she looked up at him, eyes wide, lips and fists clenched. In eagerness or fear? Either way, he'd take it slow. Like a new filly before her first ride, he'd calm her with his hands and voice before putting any weight on her.

"You hungry?" He'd eaten a light meal in the dining room while he waited.

She shook her head. Golden ripples shifted to reveal tantalizing hints of flesh.

"Tired?"

She nodded. "I didn't sleep well the last few nights."

"No one touched you, did they? You weren't afraid?" If anyone had hurt her, he'd make them pay. Only part of that was for daring to touch what was his.

"Sometimes I was a bit afraid. But even more, I was angry."

Holding the posy of wildflowers in one hand, she crossed her arms over her chest, frowning. She covered up what he ached to touch.

"And I'm still angry! Why should I be put in jail for defending myself, then forced to marry a man I've never seen before? I can make my own way with my brain and hands. But no," she dragged out the word, "all that matters to men is a woman's body. Do you think that deputy is smarter than me just because he has something in his trousers that I don't?"

Trace clenched his jaw to stop a smile from erupting. Ma had been a strong-minded woman like Beth. Pa told him to keep his opinions to himself until after he and his wife sweated on the sheets. He said women were more amenable after they'd had a few bouts of glory. His cock was so hard he'd have Beth shouting in glory all night and into the morning before he'd reply to such a dangerous comment. He had to prove to Beth that she could want his body as badly as he did hers. She had passion, all right.

"Sheriff said you read his law books."

He caught a faint blush on her cheeks. "I had to do something to keep my mind off those disreputable men. Blackstone has some interesting ideas about..." She flicked her eyes down. "I'm married to you, yet I don't even know how well you can read."

He stepped close and lifted her hand to his mouth. His elbow brushed against her nipple. She quivered.

"I told you Ma made sure of it." He whispered. Only when his breath went through his destroyed voice box did he sound like a monster. "Look at me, Kate."

"I don't use my second name. Just Elizabeth."

"But you act like a Kate. One who needs taming."

He sucked her fingertip into his mouth and bit gently as he watched her eyes. It took a moment, but he saw the instant she understood his reference to Shakespeare. Ma read every play out loud except *The Taming of the Shrew*. Pa read that one with a grin. It got Ma as flustered as a broody hen with a fox camped outside the henhouse.

"I am not a shrew and I will not be tamed!"

She glared into his eyes. He held back a smile at the way she took the bait. If their vows had included the word "obey" she was the type to cross her fingers and mumble when she spoke the words.

"According to Sheriff Chambers, Big Joe, and most of the men in this town, you are." She tried to yank her hand away but he held tight. Her nostrils flared when he touched her breast again. "I like you just the way you are, Mrs. Elliott. I tame horses. I don't want a tame wife. I want one who fights back with fire."

Her blush heated his blood. How far down did that rosy flush go? To her breasts or all the way to her belly?

"What happened to your throat? You sound fine when you whisper."

"Got roped and dragged behind a horse for a few miles. Wrecked my voice box, but I can whisper and whistle just fine."

He changed the subject by lowering his hands, and hers, so his thumbs could brush her nipples. She inhaled and thrust her chest toward him. Though he wanted to jump in, he had to make a few things clear up front.

"You're my wife, and I'm your husband. Till death do us part, Mrs. Elliott." He raised his eyebrows and tilted his head down at her to make his point. "I want respect between us. Respect and complete honesty. I expect someday we'll have a deep friendship. But don't get any womanly notions about love. It killed my pa and that won't happen to me."

"I don't need your love. I've lived without it all my life just fine."

He searched her face. She looked back, calm and sure. He might have been left an orphan at sixteen, but his parents had cared about him until then. Not as much as each other, unfortunately, but it was more than what Beth grew up with.

"According to the laws of man and God, I now own you and everything you possess. Including your body." She squawked like he knew she would, but he didn't stop. "I don't take what's not given freely." She shut her mouth, pressing her lips tight. At least the woman had enough sense to keep some of her opinions to herself now and then. "I want my wife in my bed. After tonight, I expect you'll want to be there as well. But no Elliott will force you to do anything you really don't want to do."

He chose his words carefully. He'd be able to remind her of them later when she realized what they would ask of her. Ask and encourage strongly, but not demand.

"I don't lie, Beth. Ever. I expect the same from you." She stared up at him. Emotions flashed over her face so fast he couldn't decipher them while staring deep in her eyes. "You're full of fire, Mrs. Elliott." He winked. "I like that in a wife."

"Good. I'm not changing who I am just because I had to marry you." She glanced down. "You were also forced into this."

A finger under her chin brought her eyes back to his. "Nope. No one forces me to do anything I don't want to. After I got my voice wrecked, I gave up on thinking about a wife. I told Simon and Jack they'd have to haul one home so the Elliott name would live on."

"Why would your voice matter? It doesn't change who you are."

"That's not what the few single women I've run into, and their mamas, thought." He pushed back memories of flirting women turning pale in horror when he spoke to them. His money and name weren't enough to make up for it when there were so many other men to choose from.

"Those same women would condemn me for having set foot in a jail, much less spending three days in a cell."

"Frank locked you up for your own good."

She pulled back, but he didn't let her escape. "I was minding my own business walking past the bank when I was accosted by that horrid bully, Big Joe! I was only defending myself so why wasn't *he* locked up, instead of me?"

"Joe works for the mayor, who might order him released immediately to go after you again. Putting you in a cell was the only way to keep you safe."

"Your mayor would have let Big Joe marry me, condemning me to a short, horrid life. That is not right!"

Trace nodded. "Something's strange between those two. Mayor

Rivers is as smooth as a flannel-mouthed liar but no one's caught him out yet." When Beth frowned, he realized this was no way to talk on his wedding night.

"I told Frank I'd marry any woman to keep her from Big Joe's fists." He caressed her cheek with his knuckle. "Then I saw you standing nose to nose with Charlie Newton. There you were with dirty toes, scraggly hair, and an attitude bigger than Montana Territory." He snorted a laugh and shook his head. "You, Mrs. Elliott, are my kind of woman." He grazed his thumbs against her nipples once more. A blaze lit her eyes and a moan escaped her clenched jaw.

"You're beautiful, but that can change. I want a wife with a strong backbone. One who'll live with her husband and his brothers and not give a damn what's whispered in town." He flicked her nipples again. This time she stepped closer, brushing her belly against his hard length. He bit back a needy hiss.

"Women with opinions and a fiery tongue have passion. I want that. I may not agree, but we can work it out, together."

"You mean that? You won't tell me to 'hush, woman'?"

He waggled his head, debating how to answer. Truth won out as usual. "I expect I might sometimes. But that won't stop you. I can see you got a brain and I expect you'll use it." He leaned close, nose to nose. "But don't fight with me in town. A man who can't keep his wife in line is seen as weak. I've never been weak. If you sass me, I'll have to spank you."

She reared back. "Spank me? There's no way you're ever going to do that!" She squeaked the words but her nostrils flared.

"I won't have to if you behave, wife." He purred the words, both a threat and a promise.

She pouted, her eyebrows low. He knew she'd push his limits each and every day. One day, she'd sass him in town just to see if he'd follow through. He would. He couldn't wait to haul her across his lap and paddle her right through her dress. She'd scream bloody murder, but he'd do it, even if he had to sit on the boardwalk with his feet in the mud. As soon as he got her on Elliott land, he'd do it again. This time he'd strip her naked and use the flat of his hand on her bare bottom. She'd be soaking wet by then, desperate for him to kiss her better before plunging deep.

He closed his eyes and fought for control, pulling up memories of winter blizzards and plunging in icy spring ponds. Anything to cool the raging heat demanding he take her, hard. Now!

Only when he thought he could look at her without ripping off that scrap of nothing and thrusting her against the wall, did he speak again.

"I want you to enjoy my touch, Beth. When I enter you the first time, it may hurt a bit. I'm a big man. But I'll pleasure you before and after."

His speech over, he let himself look down. Her nightgown, if that see-through cloth could be called clothing, had a line of buttons down the front, all the way to her belly. Two pink peaks, each the size of the tip of his little finger, jutted toward his chest. She was his now, and he'd cherish every inch of her. Again and again.

"You like pleasure, Mrs. Elliott?"

She looked away before shyly nodding. "I like your kisses," she whispered. A pink flush rose from her belly to her hairline. "They make me tingle."

"I'll make you more than tingle when I touch what's under those buttons." He finally let his fingers grasp her full breasts. Her moan matched his.

"Sophie said you have wicked ideas," she gasped out. "She said you wouldn't expect your wife to do what you did at Miss Lily's." She flicked her eyes up and down like a flirt, but unintentional. "She wouldn't tell me what she meant."

"You give me lots of wicked ideas, Mrs. Elliott. But Sophie's wrong." He suckled her breast, lightly scraping his teeth as he pulled back to release her. "I expect you to learn my tricks and invent a few of your own."

"Miss Lily gave me this nightgown." He narrowed his eyes when a faint smile flickered around her lips. "Sophie said if you want me to wear it again you have to undo the buttons, one by one."

His cock, already harder than an icicle in January, thickened. Dang, the woman learned fast! That was a challenge if he'd ever heard one. What was it about her that sent his temperature reeling? Was it Beth herself or the fact he had unlimited access to her voluptuous body?

He couldn't stop the growl. He locked the door, then jammed a chair against the handle just in case. Frank Chambers said he'd keep Big Joe locked up until after they left town. While the man had no friends, there were those who wanted to get in his good books. The wooden chair might not keep them from the room, but he'd be warned if they tried to break in. He removed his gun belt and placed it on the table next to the bed.

Her color deepened with every slow step he took back to her. Though he wanted to rip the gown with both hands and dive in, she was a virgin and needed to be eased into pleasure. And he wanted to see her wear that piece of fluff in their bedroom. In daylight.

"Wine?"

She nodded, thank God. Wine on a near-empty stomach would help relax her.

Nothing would make him relax. Ever since he'd seen her, he'd been harder than a railroad spike. Even if he'd spent himself in his quick but thorough bath, he'd still be hard.

She carefully placed his flowers in a water jar. She lifted it to her nose and sniffed, then set it down. She turned and accepted the glass he held out. He sipped once, then set his wine on the table. He moved behind her, eager to touch. She trembled as he gathered her hair with his fingers. Like golden silk, it was. He couldn't wait until she impaled herself on him and trailed it over his belly. It would ripple as she shuddered, her orgasm shattering her as she rode him like Lady Godiva.

He waited for her to finish her wine, then parted her hair and draped it forward. He followed its flow with his hands, over her breasts and down to her belly. Then he kissed the naked nape of her neck. She shivered. He nibbled, scraping his teeth gently and was rewarded with a moan. He reached around and plucked the empty glass out of her hand, setting it safely on the table.

He set to work on the buttons that ran from her chin to heaven. His thick fingers had to work hard to release the small pearls. Though he wanted to complain to Lily, she'd just laugh and say anticipation made the prize sweeter. Beth was sweet already. For each inch revealed, he rewarded himself with a taste of her creamy, pink skin.

He forced himself to go slowly, kneeling to reach the last few buttons. Her scent rose to him, rousing a beast he'd kept quiet too long. He pressed his tongue in her navel and scraped his teeth over her belly. Eyes glistening, nostrils flaring, she gazed down at him, clutching her gown closed like a shield.

"Show me," he choked.

It took her a minute to get her balance. She stepped back, pressed the gown off her shoulders, and released it. She clenched her hands at her sides as the gauzy fabric drifted to pool at her feet.

A groan like an animal in pain filled the room.

The fire flickered over high, proud breasts. Her soft, rounded belly called to his tongue. His heart spasmed so hard he couldn't breathe. Golden curls whisped over her pussy, tantalizing him with flashes of flesh as she shifted nervously from foot to foot.

"Closer," he croaked.

She lifted her foot high enough for him to see dew sparkling on swollen pink folds. He ground his teeth. She stopped, just out of his reach, and bit her lip.

"I can't leave that beautiful nightgown on the floor." She quickly turned and bent over to pick it up. Unknowing, she flashed him a view of paradise when her cheeks separated. A paradise he'd spend the next few dozen years enjoying. She carefully placed the nightgown over a chair and faced him again.

"Let me touch you," he growled. "Pleasure you."

Head down, she inched forward, toes gripping the rug, until he grasped her thighs. He encouraged her to spread her feet before him, opening her to his exploration. He leaned close until her fine hair tickled his nose. She smelled of sunshine and strawberries. A spring rain. An October thunderstorm.

Chaste and wild and wicked all at once.

His.

He rose to his feet and swooped her into his arms. She gasped and clutched him around the neck. He set her gently on the bed, knelt before her, and gazed down. Her large breasts, each dotted with a hard pink nipple, waited for him. When he gently urged her legs apart and bent his mouth to her, she shook her head and held her knees together.

"I'm your husband. You belong to me. All of you. As you do me."

"But—"

"But nothing. I want to taste every inch of you. I promise you'll enjoy it."

She rolled her bottom lip inside her teeth. After a moment she relaxed her thighs, closing her eyes at the same time.

He was pleased she was shy. She didn't yet know what she wanted or how to get it. It was his job to show her the pleasure a man could give a woman. Only then would he take her maidenhead, and that, gently.

This time.

He hoped there'd be times when they'd attack each other, fighting to mount, to be mounted. *Lord, let it be soon.*

He saw the thin crack between her eyelids, which proved she watched. He wanted to taste her, to make her scream his name. He stood and stripped to the waist, kicking off his boots to save time later. He knelt before the high bed, a perfect height for him. He lifted her feet and pressed the soles together so her knees spread wide, opening her up. She squeaked and fell back on her elbows but didn't complain.

He stared at her sweet pussy. He was the first to view this beautiful sight. Her white thighs spread wide, pulling her lips with them so the lamp lit up the deep pink center. She was already wet for him, but she'd be soaking the sheets before he would enter her with his cock.

Her pussy clenched as he watched, squeezing nothing. He reached forward and pressed his finger into her, just an inch. She clenched again, her muscles holding his finger tight. He looked up, catching her watching him. She jammed her eyes shut and he chuckled.

"You'll have more than my finger to hold soon enough, sweetheart."

He held her thighs up with his hands and slowly approached, nosing apart her lips. Her soft hair tickled his nose. He slid his tongue between the grooves on each side of her pussy, careful to keep his moustache from her clit. When he pressed his tongue into her, he was rewarded by a soft gasp. He inhaled deeply as if to imprint her sweet, musky scent in his brain.

He teased her apart with callused fingers and flickered his tongue over her tiny clit until it rose to salute him. She twitched her bottom, rocking her hips forward. He sucked at the top junction of her pussy lips, again flicking her rapidly swelling clit. When he pressed a finger into her, more deeply this time, she thrust back, a small moan escaping.

She lay back on the bed and lifted her hips, demanding more. The position revealed her tight brown asshole. He wet his little finger with her juices and teased the tight flesh. When he gently pressed in and released, a ring of pink appeared for a moment. *Oh, yes!* Rather than clenching tight to keep him out, she'd relaxed the ring of muscle. Her reaction suggested she would receive pleasure there, as well.

Her reaction meant there'd be more options for the Elliott men to please her. Not that they wouldn't be just as satisfied as she. But he wouldn't think about sharing her with his brothers. Tonight was all about her needs.

He pressed two fingers inside her pussy and cupped them forward, his thumb pressing against her rising bud. She gasped and arched, thrusting hard when he repeated the action. She jerked, head flipping from side to side, hands clenched into the covers.

"Oh, yes," she called, unaware she spoke. Unaware of what she asked for.

He smiled to himself and renewed his efforts with fingers, tongue, nose, and chin. Her soft body, so different from his own, wriggled before him as he found her special spots. She gasped and twitched, wanting more. Needing more.

When he knew she was close he pressed the tip of his wet thumb in her bottom. She squealed and bucked against his hand like an unbroken filly. He extended her ride until she collapsed. He stood up, watching her breasts as she panted and tiny aftershocks made her shiver.

He nibbled his way up her body, giving her a chance to find herself again. She kept her eyes closed until he plundered her mouth. He started gently, but when she pressed her hands against his head to keep him close, he thrust his tongue into her just as he wanted his cock in her sweetness. She sucked him deep, demanding more. He pulled away and backed up a few steps before he lost even more control. He hadn't been this hard and horny since his first visit to Miss Lily's Parlor.

Her eyes opened languidly. "Oh, my," she said. "I had no idea..."

"That's just a taste, my delightful wife. Are you ready for more?"

"There's more?"

He took her words as a challenge, using his fingers and tongue to bring her once again to the edge of release. But this time he slowed before completion, letting her passion dim a bit. He wanted to make her scream his name, but this time she would have to ask for more. He wanted a wife who would ask for what she wanted rather than expect him to know. He moved away and waited until she opened her eyes.

The tip of her pink tongue pressed down on her lower lip. He winked and she pouted in reply. Beth was a determined woman, but he was even more stubborn and would wait her out. He knew how to read body language. It worked with horses, poker, and fights. No reason it wouldn't work on a woman. Beth's passion was something he'd hoped for, but not expected. It meant he wouldn't have to tell her to shush. No, he'd just nibble along the side of her neck, and she'd forget what she was about to say.

His father said it worked like a charm with his strong-minded mother, not that she hadn't done the same to him on occasion. They'd loved each other far more deeply than they had their children. He wouldn't make that mistake. He and Beth could enjoy each other's bodies and company without love destroying those around them.

Loving, now that was another kettle of fish. He planned to have lots of that, starting now. She wanted more, and he'd give her such an explosion that she'd not remember the initial pain of a virgin becoming his woman.

He slowly, deliberately, unbuttoned his pants as she watched. He tossed them aside and kept going, forcing himself to do it slowly. Only his lifetime need for total control had kept him from exploding dozens of times as he pleasured her. When he finally dropped his drawers and released the hardest, largest erection of his life, it pointed to her like an enormous compass needle. She inhaled and scuttled back on the bed.

"Oh, my," she whispered. Her eyes were wide but, he thought, more in fascination than horror.

He pulled on his foreskin. A drop at the tip glistened. Staring, she licked her lips. She watched, mouth open. He pulled his sheath all the way back, his deep plum head thick and hard.

She sat up on her knees, to see better he hoped.

"If you want me, you'll have to ask," he said. "This way, I can be sure you're ready to be my wife in all ways. Once I enter you, our wedding can't be annulled."

She frowned and bit her lip. She pushed her hair behind one ear with her hand, revealing a firm breast and taut nipple.

"I want you in every way, Trace Elliott," she said, almost growling. She reached out her hand, then pulled back. "Can I touch it?"

"You can do anything you want with me, wife."

He stepped to the edge of the bed. She took him in her soft hands. His cock jumped and he immediately realized this was not a good idea. Control only went so far, and he was at his limit.

She leaned over and licked his tip.

"Whoa!" He backpedalled so fast he almost tripped over his boots. He'd damn near erupted like a geyser.

"Did I do something wrong?"

"Shh, little one," he said, fighting the urge to plunge deep into her pouting mouth. "I want you so bad I might choke you. Lean back."

She did so, heels against the edge of the mattress, knees apart. Her pussy, swollen and red from his mouth, wept for him.

"Sweetheart, are you ready?"

She touched herself with one hand, spreading her lips as he had done earlier. "This will make you my husband? No one could take me from you?"

No one was going to take her anywhere but him for a while. Not even Simon or Jack. No how, no way. Not trusting his wrecked vocal cords, he nodded.

"Then I want you now."

Her red gates clenched as if he was already there. He groaned and stepped close. He set his eager cock between her lower lips, rubbing back and forth while he massaged her breasts. He hadn't paid near enough attention to them. Her eyes widened when he squeezed her nipples between thumbs and forefingers.

"Like that, do you?"

She nodded, so he pinched a little harder. She arched her back. With his next slow thrust his dark purple head stretched her, preparing her to take all of him. He moved slowly, fighting the need to slam deep, to take her hard and fast. But this was about Beth's needs, not his own.

Another inch and he hit her barrier. He waited a moment, then pinched her clit. When she arched her back he shoved forward, breaking through. He waited, panting and trembling.

"You okay?" he growled.

She nodded. He slid in and out, just an inch or three, building her tension. She writhed, moaning and thrusting herself onto him. He caught her clit between his knuckles. She came, her internal spasms squeezing him, and all bets were off. His control, something he'd staked his life on again and again, shattered when he plunged deep inside her. He pumped hard, clasping her hips and pulling her to him as he thrust forward. Faster and faster as she keened until she clenched against him again and he exploded.

He jerked like a puppet, pumping his life into his woman.

His wife.

His future.

A slow, satisfied smile appeared on the lovely face below him. He held her hips to stay inside her until his head stopped spinning. A loud buzzing filled his ears and the room tilted. When he pulled out, still semi-hard, the tip of his cock trailed a thin line of red down her thigh.

He used cool water to wash off the evidence of her lost maidenhead. She barely opened her eyes. He scooped her into his arms and laid her high on the bed. When he lay beside her, she rolled to him, her luscious body half on top of him. He wrapped an arm around her to hold her tight, threw the covers over them with his free hand, and let the world disappear.

Chapter Five

A whisper in her dream made Beth smile lazily. She lay on her back, warm and comfy. A deep, guttural groan erupted nearby. Lips enfolded her nipple, and she arched into his touch, the dream so real. A dream that, had her parents known, would have sent her to an asylum for fallen women.

"More," she murmured.

"It's my turn, wife."

Wife? She wasn't married in her dreams—there weren't any men worth it. She opened her eyes to find dark ones laughing down at her. "You offered me something a while back."

Heat shot from her belly to her face. She shut her eyes again. Though it was low on the horizon, the full moon lit the bed.

"I know you're awake, wife."

She reached to pull the covers over her head. Though he held her wrist gently, she couldn't move.

"I have a name, you know," she groused, glaring.

He lay on his side, head propped up on his elbow, looking down at her. Grinning. She focused her attention on his wide, strong chest. She'd never been so at ease with anyone. This man, a stranger a few short hours ago, was her husband. A husband who had done such wonderful things with her. His touch, gentle or rough, made her tingle. Beside him, she felt safe and cherished, as if he really cared about her.

All her life she'd wanted to matter to someone for more than what she could provide. While she enjoyed his company, he had needed a wife and she, a husband. She didn't expect him to treat her so gently once they reached his cabin. She would enjoy what she could as long as possible and let tomorrow take care of itself.

"Yep, you're Mrs. Trace Elliott," he said. "My wife."

"My name is Elizabeth Elliott. You may, however, call me Beth."

"I'll call you whatever I want. Princess. Goddess. And sometimes Kate and a royal pain in the ass. But always, my woman."

She twitched her lip, refusing to meet his eyes. She'd never admit it, but something in her reveled in his possession of her. Of all the men she'd met, none could compare to her husband. He belonged to her now.

"I feel safe with you," she said, more to herself than her husband. "No one will hurt you again."

She saw affection and pride on his face. Not love. He'd insisted he'd never love her.

But what did she know of love? A wife was lucky if her husband didn't beat her or spend all his money on drink. She had one who wanted to please her in ways she'd never known existed. A husband who would provide her with children to love. He said respect and honesty was what kept a marriage going. She'd not known any of it growing up. So far, it felt wonderful.

She glanced farther down the bed. The object that had brought her so much delight rested on the sheet. It grew as she watched. Her breasts swelled in reaction. She remembered how satisfied she'd felt before falling asleep.

And what she'd offered.

She reached down and stroked him with her fingertips. It felt hard and soft at the same time. A dark eye peeped out of its hiding place. She scrunched down in the bed so she could grasp it with both hands. Trace murmured encouragement. He'd brought her so much pleasure with his mouth. Was that what he wanted her to do in return?

She sat up. He rolled onto his back and pressed a pillow under his head.

"You'll have to tell me what to do," she said.

"You told me you have a brain. Use it."

Trace encouraged her to break free from the repressed way she'd been raised. He was a hard, rough-living man with a voice to match. He'd never fit into a category Eastern society marked "acceptable." She knew none of the girls at Miss Primula's Ladies' College would condescend to even sniff down their noses at someone like him, even if his voice were perfect. Yet he wanted her, and she'd discovered a sensual joy with him, one she'd never imagined. Even more, she'd found a man who wanted to please her, at least in bed

She stroked him, running his cover back and forth so his organ appeared and disappeared. It grew so long it couldn't hide anymore. She grasped him in both hands, leaned over and licked the dark tip. He jerked under her grasp, but she held tight. She rolled his taste over her tongue. Salty and earthy. A drop had gathered again. She wiped it off with one finger and, watching his eyes, brought it to her mouth. She opened her mouth and slid her finger inside, slowly pumping as he had done to her a few hours ago.

"You're asking for it, woman."

His growled threat, rather than frightening her, made her bold. She turned her back, straddling him, and leaned over. She held him tight in one hand and pressed him into her mouth. He slowly pumped, her mouth making wet, sloppy sounds as he moved in and out.

She got more comfortable, leaning farther over to take him deeper. When she stopped for a breath, he pressed his fingers into her. She jerked in surprise and delight.

"Follow my lead," he said.

She did, sucking him deep when he plunged his fingers into her, flicking her tongue when he did the same to her. She widened her knees and slid back so he would have better access. Wantonly spreading her most intimate parts to him, she demanded satisfaction.

He pulled out of her grasp, growling deep. She sat up and turned around, unsure. Nostrils flaring, he eyed her like she was food and he'd been starving for years.

"Bend over. Hands and knees. Wide apart," he ordered, every word crisp.

She thought about sassing back, but he anticipated her with an upraised eyebrow. She would obey, but on her terms. She slowly did as he asked, carefully settling her knees far apart before bending forward.

He covered her, his chest snug against her back, muscular thighs pressing against the back of hers. His manhood slid under her, spreading her folds wide. He grasped her breasts, squeezing them and rasping her nipples with his calluses. He slid one hand down her belly, pressing his cock hard against her, flicking her bud with his finger.

She moved her hips restlessly, trying to make him slide his cock into her. Nothing mattered but her need for him.

He finally pressed against her, easing his way in. She responded eagerly, pushing back until his groin rested snug against her. His balls swung gently to tap her sensitive flesh.

He pulled out, dragging slowly before thrusting deeper than before. He pressed on her back, bending her forward until she rested her forehead on her fists, bottom high in the air.

"Mmm, nice," he murmured.

It was. So very nice. Long, lazy strokes stoked her engine, coal by coal. He flicked his finger against her and she clenched, the spark igniting the coal. She brought her knees closer together, the better to hold him, to increase the sensations.

He pressed a finger into her bottom. She hissed, tensing at the shallow invasion. The extra sensation broke her concentration. One hand on her breast, his cock deep in her, and now this new delight. He kept a double rhythm, cock and finger in and out. Just enough to tantalize, to grow the delicious frustration. It wasn't enough.

She rose up slightly and began moving, back and forth, controlling his thrusts.

"That's it, sweetheart. Take what you need."

She took him at his word. She slammed back against him, clenching hard. His balls slapped against her bud with every backward thrust. His finger drilled her, not deep but twisting. It wakened nerve endings, promising even more joy to learn.

She pumped, wanting more.

Her back cheek erupted with a smack of his palm. She screamed and he thrust hard. His thighs held him tight against her. Another few thrusts and she exploded. She heard distant grunts, sounding in time with her thrusts. It went on until, finally, he pulled her against his chest and collapsed sideways. She quivered, twitching, until the dark pulled her down.

* * * *

Trace held the softly snoring woman snug against him.

What the hell had he done to deserve a wife like Beth? After years on his own, raising the twins after the MacDougals took the others to Texas, he had someone to share his life with. Brothers didn't count. He, Simon, and Jack shared the work, got drunk, and fought together. He'd not known tenderness since Ma died. It caused a man to be weak. But he could be tender to his woman when she pleased him.

But Beth was an Easterner—maybe his luck hadn't changed. She could be great in bed but useless for ranch work, like Prudence MacDougal. His lip twitched at the thought of hiring an old widow to do Beth's chores while she kept her strength for the bedroom. Or anywhere else he wanted to take her.

The kitchen table. Against a few walls. On the grass in the sunshine. By the creek on the soft moss. In the creek…He swelled, again, just thinking about it. Had he gone that long without release that he was eager for more already? A new bride got sore, didn't she? He'd leave it up to Beth. He didn't care if he rubbed himself raw as long as it gave her pleasure.

He'd ordered a hot bath for the morning. He planned to wash

every delicate inch of her gorgeous body while the sun shone. He would investigate those intriguing gold-fuzzed folds hiding her womanhood. Hot baths weren't something he and his brothers worried about. A quick wash in the cold stream was the usual. But women needed a bit of pampering to keep them sweet-tempered. Pa made sure he knew about that. The older boys stoked the stove and filled its reservoir with water every Saturday night after supper. After Ma bathed the little ones, he'd fill it again before bed.

With a woman coming home, he'd better buy a few things. He might as well rent a wagon and get everything they needed for the summer. It was Simon's turn after Trace to head to town and he could return it. After all, he couldn't very well haul Beth behind him on Sailor. Not that he wouldn't mind her breasts warming his back. He'd take off his shirt and make her open her blouse. Skin to glorious skin. His cock swelled against Beth's backside. His little man had saluted more times since he saw Beth than in the last ten years.

Beth stirred. He forced thoughts of washing in the stream during early spring, the water full of snow melt. It cooled his need, temporarily.

Yep, Simon could return the wagon. At least he and Jack were allowed back in town now that he was married and all. And won't that set a fox in the henhouse.

Even covered head to toe, her golden hair braided into a crown, Beth oozed sex. Demanded it. He had to get her out of town before Big Joe saw her. All cleaned up and with that knowing, just-been-pleasured look on her, every single man and most of the married ones would be cursing his luck.

Frank told him there were two names in the mayor's hat that night—Big Joe and Old Walt. The only man with enough balls to stand up to the town bully was a grizzled prospector with a sweet tooth. He'd have Patsy give the man a box of fancy chocolates in consolation and thanks.

Thanks for trying to save Beth from Big Joe, and consolation that

Trace got her instead.

He had her to himself for now. How long did he have before his brothers demanded their share? And what if Beth refused? He wouldn't force her, so he'd have to get her used to being relaxed around them. That meant showing her even more pleasure, proving that her body craved a man's touch. Everywhere.

Hell, maybe he'd better send the twins to town together. Let them expend some frustration at Miss Lily's and leave him alone with his beautiful, sexy wife.

The moon had set, dawn not arrived. He really should be sleeping. He pulled Beth close. She sighed and snuggled back, her bottom tight against his eagerly awakening cock.

Go to sleep, he told it, and took his own advice.

* * * *

"You've got a tiny brown freckle right…here."

Trace touched his tongue tip to the beauty spot high on Beth's inner thigh. They'd bathed and eaten without leaving their room and now he explored her.

Again.

He had to teach his new wife it was nonsense to keep her body covered just because the sun was up.

Nope, if he was awake, he wanted her. He couldn't imagine a time in the next thirty years that he wouldn't want her naked beneath him, spread forward over the table or riding his brother while he entered that sweet little asshole.

The last one would take some working up to.

"I see your choice of weapon is armed and ready. Again." She pouted but her nostrils flared in invitation.

"You complaining?" He nipped her clit with his lips and she hissed, lifting her hips to him. He rewarded her with a sensuous kiss right on her button.

"Who, me? Wives don't complain, right?"

"Not when their husbands have them screaming—how many times so far?" As expected, she flushed. The knowing giggles and hearty congratulations when food and hot water were brought in earlier had Beth hiding in the bed, mortified.

"Shall I wince while walking to the mercantile, then bat my eyes at you? Sophie said Nettie Crabbe does that to all the men in the hotel dining room when she brings their food."

"She's never done it to me." He grazed her belly with his morning beard, delighted at the way her skin rippled in reaction to his touch.

"She'd better not make cow eyes at you."

"Jealous already, are you, wife?" He couldn't wait to show a clean, well-satisfied Beth off, but he'd not expected her to react the same.

"I'm not!" She pressed her lips together and glared. When her features relaxed into a cat-ate-the-cream smile, he braced himself.

"What if I smiled at a few men in the dining room, hmm?"

"I don't suggest you do that," he replied.

"Why not? Fair's fair."

"Then don't blame me if Sophie loses her hotel after I shoot all her regulars for flirting with my woman."

"Am I supposed to take that as a compliment?"

Her nipples hardened and a flush rose up her body. He pressed her legs apart and slid right into her hot center. She moaned and looked up at him with wide eyes.

"You can take it any way you want. But you are *my* woman." He thrust again. "My wife." Again, deeper. "Mine!"

He stopped her reply with his lips, thrusting his tongue as he surged into her below.

Chapter Six

"What's that?"

Sheet tight to her naked front, Beth stared at the bulky parcel in Trace's hands. When she didn't move, he tossed it onto the bed. It landed beside her with a soft thump. New string wrapped around the crisp brown paper.

"Open it and find out."

She clutched the sheet even tighter. "It's for me?"

He nodded. The morning sun lit the squint wrinkles around his eyes.

"I got it from Patsy Tanner at the mercantile last night. She fixed it to fit you so I can't take it back. It's too big in the chest for anyone but Miss Lily's gals and they like things fancier."

He tilted his head at her and rubbed his newly-shaven chin. Beth squirmed when she remembered what his chin had done to her early that morning. Heat rose from where his stubble temporarily branded her with a pink blush.

"Don't go to thinking those things or we'll never get breakfast." He rubbed his belly. "If you don't want it—"

He took a step toward the bed. Beth snatched the package away and pulled it into her lap before he could touch it. Too late, she realized she'd dropped the sheet. Ignoring his wicked grin, she dropped her hot face and untied the string.

She smoothed back the paper. She blinked, suddenly light-headed. White lace, silk ribbons, and a froth of fabric lay before her. She lifted up a lovely cream dress with small pink flowers sprinkled all over. Dark rose silk ribbons made it even fancier. She caressed a flower, then ran the back of her hand over a soft ribbon.

"It's for me?"

Trace sighed. "All you've got is an ugly gray dress. The even uglier brown one is only fit for rags." His voice rose. "Who else would I give this to? Of course it's for you!"

Beth rolled her lips and bit down. She blinked fast but the tears couldn't be stopped. She pressed her hands over her face so he couldn't see. The bed squeaked as it dipped with his weight. He lifted her present aside and hauled her onto his lap. He pressed her head against his chest and rocked her. His strong, warm arms held her snug while muscular thighs supported her own. She cried silently, throat too choked to speak.

"Don't cry, sweetheart," he whispered. He kissed the top of her head, still rocking. "Patsy Tanner was sweeping when I came past with your flowers last night. She saw you sighing over the dress before you got locked up, so I bought it. I thought you'd want something pretty."

"Oh, Trace!"

A dam let loose and she burst into sobs. That dam held back all the tears she never shed when her sisters got pretty things. She never got bright hair ribbons, lace-trimmed petticoats or fancy dresses. She didn't cry all those times they said she was too tall and loud to go to parties. Her mother and older sisters would flounce out the front door into a carriage, their practiced laughter tinkling. For the first few years she watched from her window as they left. Then she learned to wrap herself in dignity and ignore her ugly clothes. Her father wouldn't waste good money when she'd only get dirty doing chores. She had no beaus so didn't need fripperies.

But this man, her husband, thought of her first. He got her a store-bought dress before taking care of his own comfort. He thought about what *she* wanted and made it happen. No matter what, she would do whatever she must to be a good wife to him.

"Dammit, Beth. I thought you'd like it." She moved with his chest as he inhaled deeply, and then sighed. "Shit. Shows what I know about women."

His self-condemning words broke through her remembered pain. Her sobs turned into hiccups. "But I do," she said between gasps.

"You like my present?"

She lifted her face to him and nodded. He exhaled, dropping his forehead against hers. "Women," he muttered. "Cry when they're happy. Cry when they're sad." He lifted his head. His face looked blurred due to her tears. "This is a happy cry?"

She nodded, trying to smile.

"Good." He reached out a long arm and snagged the towel he used to dry her off earlier. He dabbed at her tears.

"I don't remember the last time I got a present," she said between hiccups.

"Well you better get used to it. My wife gets the best I can give." His hand rose and caressed her breast. She shivered at his soft touch. "I want you to feel good, inside and out." He pinched her nipple lightly. She inhaled and thrust into his hand. He chuckled.

"This present isn't just for you, sweetheart. All those men who wouldn't stand up to Big Joe and put their name in the mayor's will be cursing when they see you. They can look all they like but you're mine."

She moaned when his lips touched hers. He kissed her gently and then broke contact. She gasped when he stood and dropped her on the bed.

"Save that for later. I'm hungry and I want to show off my pretty wife."

Beth climbed off the bed and smiled at her gift. She lifted each precious piece and laid them on the bed, one by one. Bodice, petticoats, stockings, and dress.

"You forgot drawers," she said. He snickered. She turned to him and frowned at his cocky grin. "You *purposely* missed drawers!"

"You won't need 'em." He waggled his eyebrows. "I got *plans,* wife."

He stepped close. She looked up into his laughing eyes. He slid his hand over her belly. One finger eased between her legs, rubbing against her clit. She pressed her thighs apart to encourage more.

"My wife is a wanton hussy." He stroked her wetness. "Yep. Drawers get in the way." He smacked her bottom with his palm, laughing when she squeaked in response. "Stockings, boots, and one petticoat. That's it."

"I can't wear a dress with nothing underneath!"

"Why not?"

"Everyone will be able to see these." She pointed to her hard nipples. "They stick out when you're near me."

"Yep, they do." They tightened even more as his eyes caressed her. "Is that a problem?" His bland face didn't fool her.

"I'm not leaving this room with only one layer of cloth between me and the world." She crossed her arms, hiding his view. His belly rumbled loudly. He rubbed it and finally nodded.

"Wear your blue coat. But once we leave town, it comes off."

* * * *

Beth stirred her tea, careful the silver spoon didn't scratch the precious flowered teacup. She was the only woman sitting in the dining room. She felt unsettled from the way air swept past her nakedness as they walked down the stairs. He escorted her to a table and, when they sat, his leg rested against hers under the table as if staking his claim.

All during the meal, anytime she accidently caught a man's eye, he nodded courteously. She sighed. A few whiskey-laced words over a black book and her status changed from slattern to honorable wife.

"Ah, yes," said Trace loudly. "That's what a man needs after a busy night and morning."

He pushed back his second plate of breakfast with a sigh and patted his stomach. He stretched his legs under the table, jostling her in the process. He winked, eyes smiling in a way she'd already learned meant he wanted her for more than conversation. Her breasts tingled, already swelling to receive his touch.

When they rested in each other's arms and talked early that morning, she told him about her worries of fitting in. Trace said that in the West, respect had to be earned. Finding gold helped, but he and his brothers had strong fists and a quick draw. Therefore, they had high standing in town. He said he didn't care what anyone thought, that Elliotts always carried themselves with pride. He winked and said she'd fit in just fine.

She muttered that it would be the first time. He overwhelmed her with kisses at that point. Twelve hours since they married and already he knew how to control her. One touch of his hand—even one look— and she melted.

Trace was nothing like any man she'd ever met. That in itself was a problem. She couldn't figure him out as he didn't react as expected. The only thing she was sure he'd do was reach for her as soon as they were alone. Or not, she mentally added, remembering the deep kiss she received just inside the dining room. She swatted him on the chest when she recovered. He grinned like a boy caught sneaking a cookie, proud and eager for more.

Holding back a smile in memory, Beth picked up her teacup and sipped from the delicate china. By this afternoon, she'd have her own kitchen. It might be just a table in a dark, cramped cabin, but it would be hers. She knew nothing about her new home, not that she had any choice. But no matter what, she'd finally have a real home. One where she belonged and could stay forever.

Trace nudged her leg. He winked when she looked up. She pretended to be irritated, but she felt like they belonged together. No one else had ever treated her like this, teasing her, knowing she was secretly proud though pretending embarrassment.

"There's no need to boast." She kept her voice low, only for his ears.

"Sweetheart, I'm not boasting," he croaked at full volume. "I'm stating a fact. What was it, six times? Seven? Dang, I could hardly keep up with you, wife."

"I am going to kill you for that," she bit out between tight lips.

He erupted in a harsh croak, what she'd learned was a laugh.

"Slowly. Painfully." She set her teacup in its matching saucer and continued, her voice rising. "I'm thinking poison. Something that will wither your manhood and make it fall off."

"You tell him," called Old Walt from the corner. "I'm the only man with enough balls to put my name in the mayor's hat." The grizzled prospector gave a gap-toothed grin. "Figured if Big Joe kilt me, least I'd die happy."

Old Walt cackled as roars of approval erupted from the men in the dining room. Beth played along, groaning theatrically and dropping her head in her hands. The old man was kind to her. He brought a checkers board and they played through her cell bars while he told her stories of the old days.

She looked up when Trace rose to greet an equally huge man. He had an ugly slash mark across one cheek. Tendons rose from their forearms when they shook hands. The man finally gave in with a wince. In return he slapped Trace hard on the back in congratulations. Trace glared but the man laughed.

"Beth," growled Trace, "this here's Luke Frost. He and his partners have the Circle C north of town. Luke, this is my wife, Beth Elliott."

"Pleased to meet you this fine morning, Mrs. Elliott." Luke took off his hat and bowed to her. She returned his nod. "Dang, but you are a lovely sight. The one time I'm a day late getting to town this curly wolf snaps you up. Is it too late to switch husbands? My ranch partners aren't as ornery as those Elliotts." He gave her a woeful grimace, his scar pulling at his skin. Crinkles around his dark eyes proved he was joking.

She laughed, more at Trace's proprietary glare than Luke's chagrin.

"Sheriff wants a word with you," said Luke to Trace. "I'll entertain your lovely wife while you're gone."

"I bet you will." Trace sighed. He turned to her. "Can you put up with this varmint?" She nodded. "Don't believe a thing he says." Trace bent down, a wicked look in his eyes. He pulled her close and gave her a thorough kiss, bringing roars from those nearby. Adjusting his hat, he sauntered out of the room leaving Beth flushed, knees tight together.

"That man never does a thing by halves," said Luke. He dropped into the empty chair with a sigh, hat on his lap. He shook his head, pouting like a hound dog that just missed out on a juicy bone. "When I tell Gabe and Oscar how we missed marrying the prettiest woman in Tanner's Ford, they'll howl in misery." He sighed as if the weight of the world held him down. "Sure you won't consider trading husbands, ma'am? A lovely wife like you would make my life complete."

"Mr. Frost, you put the great tragedy actors to shame with that performance."

He laughed. "Can't blame a man for trying."

"I'm a happily married woman."

"So I heard." He raised his eyebrows and winked. "Seven times, was it? I had the room next door."

Heat flooded her face. She arranged her teaspoon so it rested against her saucer just so. "A gentleman wouldn't mention such a thing."

"He might if he was jealous." Luke leaned forward. "Take it as a compliment, my dear lady. I've known Trace a few years now and never seen him act this way. He's a good man and I wish you well."

"Thank you."

She sat quietly for a minute while Luke twitched in his chair.

"If I may be so bold, ma'am…"

"You have something more to say?" Thinking he was still

pretending, she acted the part of a high society matron forced to accept a ruffian in her salon.

He leaned forward, both elbows on the table, chin in his hands. "If the Circle C bagged a few turkeys, would you cook 'em? We haven't had decent roast turkey since we left home."

"Mr. Frost…"

"Ma'am, we're just a trio of banged up old soldiers. I got this," he pointed to his scar, "Oscar's blind in one eye and Gabe, well, he says so little we're not sure what happened. Seeing a lovely woman putting food on the table would brighten our miserable life."

"You really must consider theatricals, Mr. Frost."

"Grub is serious business to us bachelors, ma'am."

Beth looked straight at him. While he played a part, his words were true.

"You must discuss your flowery request with Mr. Elliott. Should he agree, I would be pleased to cook a turkey dinner for you."

Luke sat up and nodded his thanks. He flicked his eyes toward the door, then rose to his feet. Stepping near, he picked up her hand and bent over, slowly bringing it to his lips. He grinned the whole time. She heard Trace roar toward them, huffing like a locomotive. Luke released her just as Trace arrived.

"Keep your hands off my wife, Frost."

"I merely thanked the lady for her kind offer."

Trace glared at Beth. "I told him he'd have to ask you first." Trace glared even harder. She sighed at the two squaring off. "Mr. Frost wants a Sunday dinner invitation. Roast turkey, with him providing the birds."

"Dinner."

"Yep. What did you think I meant, Elliott?"

After a tense moment Trace laughed. He slapped Luke so hard on the back the man had to take a step to gain his balance.

"Guess I can't blame a man for wanting his wife to himself during his honeymoon," said Luke. He settled his hat back on his head.

"What'll the boys do when you come waltzing home with your lovely bride? You set up an account at Lily's yet?" He dropped his voice, but not low enough that she couldn't hear. "Or will you teach her to share? That's what I'd do if I had a wife." He nodded to Beth, replaced his hat, and strode toward an empty table at the back of the room, calling out for Nettie to bring him hot food.

Teach her to share? Did Trace expect her to provide female comfort to his brothers as well as cooking and cleaning for them? She knew the Bride Trains had started because there were hundreds of single men for each available woman in the West, and too many women unable to marry in the East.

Could she do *that* with another man? If Trace made her feel so wonderful, could it be even better with his brother? An odd flutter make her belly quiver. Odd because it should not happen at the thought of someone other than her husband touching her.

Beth pushed back her chair, face burning at the words she was not supposed to overhear, as well as her improper reaction. Trace helped her to stand, saying nothing. He silently held out his arm and escorted her from the dining room. As soon as they cleared town, she had a list of things to ask her new husband. For now, she'd enjoy the sunshine, her freedom, and new clothes.

Once they left Sophie McLeod's hotel, he tucked her arm under his to keep her close. They strolled along the scarred wood boards as if on the finest street in New York City. He kept to her right, both to protect her from the street and to ensure easy access to the gun resting low on his left hip.

A mild wind followed them down the street. The cool air blew up between the boards under her feet and filled her skirt. She gasped when it billowed out, swirling around her naked belly and nether regions.

"Think of what I'm going to do to those parts of you. It'll warm you right up," said Trace.

Her body immediately responded, flooding her with heat. "You are a wicked man," she murmured.

"Yep. And there'll be more later. First I'll lift your—"

"Hush!"

He chuckled but fell silent.

Saturdays the population swelled as scores of men descended on the town, eager for the comforts of beer, warm food, and hot women. Most stopped in the shacks outside the town limits as strangers weren't allowed firearms in Tanner's Ford. A few left their gun belts in the jail to get a hot bath and shave. The thought of being served by a pretty girl lured many to Sophie's dining room. When it grew dark, Miss Lily's Parlor and Baldy's Saloon did a good business.

By dark she'd be home, starting her new life with her husband and his two brothers. She prayed the cabin had more than one room. Earlier that morning, Trace said he'd have to corral the horses until they got used to her screams. She couldn't bear the thought of Trace doing those things to her with their bed screened only by a thin curtain. The loud snores and smells of men kept her awake on the train. How could she sleep with three grown men in the same room?

Later. She put the future where it belonged and concentrated on their stroll. Trace doffed his hat to the ladies and nodded at the men. She noticed him glaring at a few who grinned too broadly at her.

"You're enjoying this." She spoke between teeth clenched in a smile.

"Yep."

"Why? Everyone's staring at us."

"So what? I've been stared at ever since I got my neck roped. No," he continued after a moment's hesitation, "since the seven of us were orphaned. But it's a bright sunny morning. Instead of working, I'm showing off my beautiful new wife. For once, every man is damn jealous."

After the way she'd been ogled in jail, she understood exactly what his quiet words meant. She wanted to show him off as well. She pulled him close, slowing her steps to sway her hips.

"Now you're teasing," he whispered.

"Perhaps," she replied. "But am I teasing you, me, or the rest of the town?"

He stopped and pulled her into his arms. At first he kissed her tenderly. But the chaste kiss soon erupted into the wild abandon they'd shared last night, at sunrise and again, after their bath. When he lifted his head for air, she grabbed on to him to keep herself vertical as the buildings spun around her.

"Best you get your wife home quicksmart, Trace Elliott, afore she does something you'll be ashamed of. She needs to learn her place!"

Mrs. Emslow ran a very strict boardinghouse for single men. She ruled her boardinghouse with a moral fanaticism. Though the place was clean and the food excellent, few men stayed long as they inevitably broke one of her numerous rules. Maurice Lumley, the officious hotel clerk, was the only regular. The woman had looked down her nose at Beth for riding the Bride Train. Even marrying an upstanding member of the community rather than Trace Elliott wouldn't make up for Beth's time in jail.

"My wife will never shame me, Mrs. Emslow," growled Trace. "She's already learned where her place is. At my side." He dropped his voice. "And anywhere else I want her."

Mrs. Emslow gasped, holding her white-gloved hand over her massive bosom. She gifted them with her best glower and harrumph. She lifted her skirts and swept them aside, looking down to make sure Beth's new dress didn't touch her own, and sailed past. Beth's good spirits dimmed at the obvious snub.

"Always thought that woman's pursed lips looked like the back end of a chicken," said Trace calmly.

Beth burst into laughter. He rewarded her with a smile and wink. They reached the mercantile without further problems. Trace nodded to the old men gossiping in the morning sun. An equally ancient hound dog opened one lazy eye as Trace escorted her inside Tanner's Mercantile.

Beth inhaled the mix of tobacco, leather boots and belts, fresh-ground coffee, sour pickles, spices, and everything else that filled the store. The ceiling was high enough that her head didn't brush against the hams, slabs of bacon and cooking pots hanging from the rafters. She automatically veered to the right where bolts of material filled wooden shelves right to the ceiling. The royal blue velvet was still there, waiting for some lucky soul.

Patsy Tanner hadn't objected to Beth sighing over the fabric during her first few days in town. Though she wasn't interested in fashion, Beth had used her needle on most of her sister's dresses. When her father sold the farm and hauled her home, they couldn't afford seamstresses. She'd taken apart her sisters' dresses and put them back together, mixing and matching to make new fashions. As most everyone else was in the same tight straights, no one mentioned it. Before she was put in jail, she'd sketched out a few gowns on Patsy's carefully ironed paper, fashions that might never reach town.

But this time she kept her eyes down, hands tightly clasped so she wouldn't touch anything. While Trace had bought her everything but her newly shined boots, it didn't mean he had any cash. Spring was an expensive time, with seed and equipment needing to be bought. She understood pride and would never ask for something her husband would feel obligated to provide. Wearing new clothes was enough of a wonderful thing.

"Morning, Mrs. Tanner," said Trace. "This here's my wife, Mrs. Elliott."

"Morning yourself, Trace. It's about time you got yourself a smart woman. Elizabeth and I are already friends."

"Good." He handed the storekeeper his order list. "John out back?"

At her nod, Trace kissed Beth's cheek, murmured something to Patsy, and quietly ambled through the store and out the back door.

"We came here just after the Elliotts and MacDougals," said Patsy. "Those two families had twelve boys and two girls between them. We watched them grow. Trace was a rapscallion but he grew into a good boy. I hope you realize you're a lucky woman."

Beth nodded. She held back a smile at the spry older woman calling her huge husband a boy.

"As the only woman on the Rocking E, you'd better sew a few nightshirts first thing." Patsy winked and began pulling down bolts of fabric, some far too soft and feminine for men to wear. Beth blushed at the reminder of his brothers. She'd be mortified if they heard her cries, but she didn't want to give up the glorious pleasure she'd just discovered.

When Trace returned through the back room, Beth and Patsy sipped cups of tea, bolts of fabric and notions piled all over. He kissed her cheek, picked up her cup, and swallowed the last of her tea before looking at the counter.

"Missed something, sweetheart."

She flushed, thinking he was making a sarcastic comment at the amount waiting for his approval. "We put all that out so you could choose what you want. Mrs. Tanner said you and your brothers need nightshirts."

"Nope. Just work shirts."

He pointed to a bolt of heavy blue cotton, another of ticking. He piled three flower-sprigged bolts on top, one red, one blue, and one spring green. Then he pointed high on the wall.

Beth gulped. He couldn't be pointing to the royal blue velvet she'd spent hours thinking about while in jail. Just how she'd drape it, what the bodice would be like. While shivering in the dark, she decided which lace trim to use, gold or silver. Since it was all in her head, she'd gone with the expensive gold, to match her hair.

"That's what I thought," said Patsy with a nod. "Suits her coloring perfectly. There's some gold lace that would edge it beautifully."

"Oh, Trace, no," she said, tearing up at the thought of her small dream coming true. His name slipped out so easily she didn't notice she'd used it.

"Oh, Beth, yes," he growled in reply.

"But it's so dear. What will your brothers think?"

Patsy began humming loudly. She rolled the ladder over and climbed high. Trace hunched down and kissed Beth, uncaring who might walk in. She held him tight, squeaking when he molded her breast with his hand. She panted when he pulled away and leaned his forehead against hers.

"Jack and Simon will say you're worth it. With all of us to take care of, you'll need something special to wear now and then."

"But there's nowhere I can wear it. It's too proud for church and the dirt floor of the cabin would get it dirty in no time."

"You'll wear it for me," he replied. He held up one finger and tapped her nose with it. "But no more than three buttons. I want easy access to my wife."

A couple of hours passed before they left town. Sheriff Chambers stopped Trace to tell him that Big Joe was still in jail, sleeping off his drunk from the night before. Beth might see him again when visiting town, but she'd be surrounded by Trace and his brothers. If the man even looked sideways at her, they'd warn him off.

Sophie handed Trace a packed lunch basket for the way home and gave her a hug. She didn't yet know how to cook over a campfire, but she had lots of experience with a cook stove. Trace didn't ask if she could cook so she hadn't volunteered the information. With Patsy's encouragement, she added enough fixings to their order to surprise "her" men. Simon and Jack wouldn't be telling stories about bad cooking when they came to town.

She gritted her teeth and faced straight ahead as they passed the shacks west of town. She didn't understand some of what the men and painted women called out but what she did, was bad enough. Trace answered with growls and gestures that no one could mistake. Would this have been her life once Big Joe finished humiliating her?

Once the shacks were behind, he sat up straight. She didn't think it unusual that he kept a rifle at his feet. When she left the train in

Dillon, she'd traveled inside the stage. She was bounced around so much she had no chance to look out the window. Trace continually looked around, alert to anything out of the ordinary. She had little idea what that would be, as almost everything looked strange to her. After leaving the crowded East, the train passed through wide empty spaces. All she remembered of Dillon and Bannack City were filthy streets full of men swearing and hollering. There might be manure on the dusty streets of Tanner's Ford but the air was cleaner than her home city, the Bride Train's hard seats or any place in between. She tilted her head back and let the sun kiss her face. Whatever happened later, she'd enjoy her life today.

She recognized most of the birds singing and some of the wildflowers they passed. She relaxed, waving away the occasional insect that buzzed near. Now and then Trace's thigh brushed against hers as the wagon rattled along.

"Oh, my," said Beth after a while. She turned her head and blinked at her husband. After a moment Trace looked down at her, one eyebrow raised.

"Something wrong?"

Beth shook her head. "No. It's just that…I'm happy." She smiled up at him. "I wondered what it would feel like. Now I know."

Trace snorted like a horse and shook his head. After a moment he checked their back trail, ignoring her. Beth didn't care. She settled herself on the hard bench and watched her new world go by. An eagle soared high above. Hunting a mate, or dinner?

"How come you say you're happy now and not last night? You sure enjoyed that."

Familiar heat surged up Beth's chest to her face. She groaned when he chuckled. If she browned her face in the sun, would he know when she blushed?

"Last night in the hotel was beyond anything I could even have dreamed," she said quietly.

"There's more to learn and enjoy, Mrs. Elliott. Lots more."

"I'm not talking about that! Well, not just that." She waited until he settled again. "Last night, while I soaked in a hot tub, you went out and picked flowers for me. You bought me this beautiful dress." She spread her hands over her legs, caressing the fabric. "No one ever thought of me unless they wanted something. But you did, even before eating or bathing. It's been years since I dreamed about someone caring for me." She shook her head. "I thought no one who was that good to me, could be real."

"Sweetheart, soon's we get on Elliott land. I'll prove how real I am."

He was quiet as he guided the wagon around a rock outcrop. The butterflies that rose to flutter in her stomach at his words, settled once more.

"I know nothing about your family except they treated you like a servant or worse. But you're an Elliott now and my wife. If there's something bothering you, then it affects me."

Her heart, already touched by his thoughtfulness, softened. Though she'd done so much for him while they were children, even her brother Timothy put his own needs first. When he helped her escape from her locked room while everyone was out at a soiree, she thought he'd saved her from an abusive marriage to Abraham Carter to help her. Only later did she find out the debt her father owed Carter was from illegal activity. Timothy planned to take over the family bank. Carter had links to crime, links that her brother did not want. While Timothy might be fond of her, he'd saved her for his own reasons, not hers. Though he'd given her money to sew into her dress, it was only a portion of what was rightfully hers.

Could she let down her guard with the near-stranger sitting beside her? Had he done those things to care for her or for his own reasons? She thought he had no money but he bought her a dress and bonnet. That could be to show off his new his wife, but no one but she and Sophie would have known about the flowers. He had bought the lovely blue velvet for her but said she must make it so he could enjoy her body.

Purposely testing for a reaction, she curled her arm around his. He immediately sat up straight, his entire body stiffening. After a moment, he lifted both arms and lightly tapped the horses. The movement forced her to release him. He coughed and turned away. She waited, biting her lip and body tense, until he spoke.

"What I mean is," he said. He cleared his throat and hunched over, staring between the horses. "If you're all bothered about something, you might get sick. Now that I got me a wife, I want her in good shape. I expect a decent supper on the table when I get home and a willing woman in my bed. That's why a man takes on a wife. Good food, a tidy home, and a warm bed."

Of course. He wanted to take care of her because otherwise he might be inconvenienced. Just like her brother. How silly of her to think otherwise. When Sophie handed her the picnic basket that morning, she'd warned the honeymoon would be over when they arrived home. There was too much hard work for everyone, and no time for foolishness, she'd said to Beth.

So Beth kept her head high and fought back girlish tears as the wagon rumbled along. At least she had wonderful memories of last night and this morning. That was something no one could ever take away from her. She inhaled the warm, fragrant air. When she exhaled, she sent her foolishness with it.

Her husband was a man just like any other. Women had dreams while men had plans. Plans were real while dreams floated away with the morning mist. *Forget that he wants you for a beddable servant. Think what you'd be doing if Big Joe married you last night.* She'd be dead. One way or the other, by his brutal fists or her own hand.

With that perspective, life was good. Satisfaction, Miss Primula said, was realizing one was content with what one had. She had a decent husband, a home, a respected place in society, and, soon she hoped, children to love. The sun was shining and she was warm and dry. She could be happy with that.

They rode on for another hour, saying nothing. As Trace slowly relaxed, so did she. Neither of them returned to the way they were before he stated what he wanted out of her. If she couldn't have his heart and soul, she could have the rest of him.

Other men took what they wanted from a woman, then tossed her aside. When Trace gave her pleasure before his own, it showed he cared about her. She'd never known of the joy he gave her body. That alone was more than enough to base a marriage on. Already, she craved his touch.

His leg bumped against hers as the wagon rocked. The touch sparked the slow fuse inside her. She straightened up on the hard seat and pushed her shoulders back as if stretching. Trace glanced down at her breasts. Only one layer of thin fabric covered her skin. It rasped against her nipples, tightening the buds. A quick glance down proved his need swelled as well.

He didn't have to love her to make love *to* her. Something they both enjoyed. Years of haggling at the farm taught her honey made a better lure than vinegar. If he wanted to be the big man ordering her around, then she'd play her part to get what she wanted.

"Thank you for the velvet. It's a lovely bride present," she said. Once more she flexed her back as if she had an itch between her shoulder blades. It caught his eye.

"That's no present. It's just for because. I ordered your present. Won't be in for a while."

He lifted an eyebrow when he turned to her. She saw the fire in his dark eyes, barely banked though they'd left their bed only a few hours before.

"May I ask what it is?"

"I ordered one of those big copper bathtubs. Ma had one, but I gave it to Gillis MacDougal when he and Pru got hitched. Never thought we'd have a woman to need it."

"But they're so dear. I can have sponge baths in front of the stove when your brothers are somewhere else—"

He cleared his throat. She shut her mouth with a snap.

"It's also for me. Saturday nights I'm going to wash every inch of you. Slowly." He nodded. "So don't go thinking it's anything special."

She looked out at the scenery, remembering how he'd washed, dried, then kissed her that morning. He'd branded her breasts, belly, and thighs with the tip of himself before plunging deep and filling her with his seed. Seed that one day, God be willing, would bring her children to love.

When the horses started up a long stretch, straining to pull, she decided it was safe to bring up a subject that would not make him happy.

"There's something I have to tell you."

"You wore drawers under your dress? That's a spanking offence, Mrs. Elliott."

She flushed, both at the idea that she'd disobey his direct order on the first day of their marriage and his threat. She had no idea why the thought of a spanking had her hot and bothered and didn't want to think about it.

"It's important," she said. He shrugged. "You spent a lot of money this morning."

"I bought what my wife needs to do her job."

"Before I left home I sewed twenty-dollar gold coins into my bodice. Two of them."

He shot her a look before staring ahead again. She twisted her hands, unsure of his reaction. By law, it was his money now. She waited but he didn't speak.

"I want to help. The forty dollars is just a down payment. My brother Timothy said when I married, he'd send the money my grandmother left me. I don't know how much it is, but—"

"Keep it. Elliotts don't need money from a woman."

"You're too proud to accept help from your wife?"

"Damn straight!"

"Well, listen up, mister. I'm an Elliott now. And *this* Elliott wants to become part of your life with more than her body." Her voice wavered, but she continued. "You can buy a woman at Miss Lily's Parlor any time. You can hire someone else to cook and clean."

He hunched his shoulders, staring straight ahead.

"I need to know I'm more than a body to be used for work and your pleasure. The ranch you work on is my life now, and I want to be part of it. Big or small, it doesn't matter. Maybe we can buy enough boards to add on a bedroom for us, or for our children, if we're blessed."

It was too late to change anything. She was married to him until one of them died. But their whole life would be based on his reaction. Did he want her for herself, Elizabeth Katherine James Elliott, for everything she could give him? Or did he want Mrs. Trace Elliott, a wife who met his daily needs?

Her father threw her out of her home, forcing her to care for his parents' broken-down farm. Then he'd tried to sell her as a virginal wife to advance his business. That life was over. She needed to belong to this one. To know *she* owned a part of her home, however small.

The uneasy silence continued. The horses strained, stretching their necks to pull up the slope. Trace glowered so much she didn't offer to get out and walk to lighten their burden. Instead she looked at the unfamiliar plants, wondering what uses they could be put to. Which added flavor to food and which would give her stubborn husband the trots if dropped in his stew bowl?

"You're not just a body to be used," he finally growled. "You're my wife." He didn't look at her.

"And what does a wife have to offer, other than her body? Men don't care if a woman has a brain or any learning. They want her for chores, bedding, and heirs."

"What I want from you, most women would refuse." He finally looked at her but his hat shaded his face.

"You said you wanted me to think." He nodded, warily. "I *think* you should let me buy a part of my home."

She held tight to the buckboard as they crossed a stream, the water high from the spring melt. They crested the hill. He directed the horses under a broad cottonwood tree by the water and slowed the horses to a stop.

She waited, still and unmoving, until he sighed. Heavily.

"We don't need the gold." He sighed again. "I'll talk it over with the boys. When Ben comes, he can write up a paper to give you part ownership of the Rocking E like the rest of us."

"Ownership?"

"We work darn hard, but the Rocking E belongs to us. No banker or foreman tells us what to do."

"I wondered how you could buy all the things in the wagon."

She pressed her hand to her pounding heart. He offered far more than she'd ever expected. A real home. If her name was on the deed and anything happened to him, she could not be kicked off even if his brothers hated her. Despite his comments, perhaps he did care for her, but was afraid to show it. Her body, tingling from his nearness, heated even more. Someday he might learn to care about her as a person. For now, she could enjoy his body.

"Will that suit, Kate?"

The sarcastic way he used the name set fire to her.

"Kate?" Now that the wagon had stopped she stood up to gain the advantage. "You think I'm being a shrew by offering my money? I can do a lot worse, Mr. Trace Elliott."

His lip twitched, just a bit, but she'd learned to read his body language enough to see he'd relaxed from a few minutes ago.

"'Why there's a wench. Come on, and kiss me, Kate,'" he quoted.

She squeaked when he grabbed her waist and hauled her onto his lap. He pulled off her new pink bonnet and tossed it into the wagon. He slid his hands through her hair, pulling out her pins and undoing her careful work. When her hair floated in the breeze, his eyes burned into hers as his nostrils flared. Her nipples pebbled, knowing what he wanted.

"Conclusion of act five, scene two. 'Come, Kate. We'll to bed.'" He looked around. "In this case, 'we'll to wagon.'"

Chapter Seven

"What if someone sees us?"

Trace's luscious new wife stood on the grass beside the wagon, staring up at him. She licked her lips, and he held back a moan. That tongue, though untutored, already drove him wild when she sucked him dry. The woman grew on him like a rash, taking over more of his life every minute. He'd almost lost it when she said he couldn't be real because he treated her as if she mattered.

Imagine him, Trace Elliott, wanting to hug a woman because she was more alone in the world than he was. She said no one cared about her. Worse, she'd stated it as a fact rather than a complaint. He'd almost let her into his heart before he realized the danger.

She was his wife. He'd protect and provide for her. She would serve his needs, in bed and out, as well as those of the twins. Between them they'd raise their children on the Rocking E. They had a partnership with intriguing benefits. And he wanted some right now.

"Mr. Elliott?"

Her golden hair rippled in the light breeze. She stood on Rocking E grass, waiting for him. When she screamed his name on Elliott land, she would belong to them fully. Her joy would echo off the mountains around them. Then he'd take her home.

Soon, every inch of her, inside and out, would be his. Only then would he share her.

She bit her lip and frowned as she stared at him. Was she really nervous about baring her entire body to the sun? Or did she only need his encouragement to give in to her wanton streak.

As soon as they passed the shacks outside Tanner's Ford, she'd removed her coat. He gave her a few moments to settle before insisting she undo her shirt collar. The curve of creamy flesh drew his eye constantly, jiggling with every step the horses took.

He was a saint for waiting until now to haul her into his arms.

He drew his finger between the swell of her breasts. He licked her sweat off his finger, sucking it as she had his cock that morning. She inhaled, nipples already hard for him.

"Anyone could see us."

"No one can see you here," he replied.

Her tight shoulders relaxed.

"Other than Simon or Jack."

"What?"

"Sy might be scouting a bee tree up there." Trace pointed to the mountains before them. "The man has a sweet tooth. Jack's likely hunting the other side of the ridge." He turned back to Beth. "If Sy's up there, he'll have his spyglass out."

Beth interlaced her fingers across her middle. He'd easily learned how to tell her arousal, but there was something else going on. She'd jumped to her feet, face red, as soon as Luke left their table. Had she heard his comment? She'd been twitchy since they left town.

"Something you want to say?" he asked.

She nibbled her lip, looking down. Her fingers were clenched so tight they were white.

"What did Mr. Frost mean about teaching me to share?"

"Heard that, huh?"

He winced when she nodded, still not looking at him. He gathered her in his arms. She resisted at first but he held her tight until she gave in. Her heart pounded against his chest.

"You know I live with two of my brothers?" He felt her nod against his chest. "Since Ma and Pa died and the MacDougals took the four youngest away to Texas, all we had was each other. We shared everything, work, food and shelter, and managed to stay alive. All along, each of us hoped that some day one of us would marry and keep the Elliott name alive here in Montana Territory."

He kissed the top of her golden head. She trembled but didn't pull away.

"I married you. A strong, determined woman full of passion." He ran his fingers over the outer curve of her breast. A hard nipple rose, pressing against his chest.

"I won't force you to do anything you really don't want to do, Beth. But Simon and Jack have needs, just like me." He waited a few moments for her to think it over. She didn't move. Her pounding heart didn't slow down, either. He didn't think she was ready to bolt, so he relaxed his hold a mite.

"I want you. Here and now. If Sy is watching, he wants you too." He cupped her swollen breast. He heard the quiet hitch in her throat, the one that meant she wanted more.

"Don't think about what might happen, Beth. Think about how good you feel when I touch you." He caught her nipple between his fingers. When he squeezed, she whimpered.

"Maybe Sy saw the wagon dust. He hauls out his spyglass and sees me holding a beautiful woman. He wonders if you're a mirage or the daydream of a man who's gone without a woman for six months. Does it make you hot, thinking my brother watches you, wishing he was the one touching you?" She pressed her face against his shirt making a hot circle from her breath.

"This is the next step to becoming an Elliott wife. Me loving you out in the open on Elliott land. I'm going to strip you naked. Then I'll lick the sweat off your skin and suck your sweetness until you explode. And when I lay you down and fill you with my seed, Sy will imagine he is the one spreading your thighs and making you scream. Only it'll be my name that echoes over the land."

She twitched with the tiny shivers that meant she wanted him. But she was a woman and had been raised with notions as to what was seemly. Notions he would stretch until they broke. He'd made a good start last night and this was the next step.

"But—"

"Kate, if you don't show me your sweet ass by the time I count to three, I'm going to lift your skirts and paddle it!"

She pushed on his chest and stared up at him, her mouth moving like a fish out of water. She snapped her lips closed and raised her chin. She shoved him away.

"You wouldn't dare!"

"Never dare an Elliott, sweetheart." He couldn't resist a slow smile of anticipation. "One," he said. He moved to the back of the wagon where they'd left an open space. He lifted himself and settled in the middle.

"Two." He reached his arms wide to ensure there was enough room to lay her across his lap. He patted his thighs to show where she'd lie, face down.

"Stop! You win."

She pursed her lips and glowered like Mrs. Emslow. But her look did things to him the old besom would never understand. He leaned back on his hands with a broad smile, feet swinging, to watch her undress. When she reached for the next button over her chest, he stared at her fingers, anticipating the view. She slowly flicked the button open, then the next. Another one and the curve of her breast appeared. He'd fought hard for her to go with undergarments. This made it worthwhile.

She touched the next button, caressing it. She opened her mouth and touched the tip of her tongue to her top lip. He swallowed, waiting for what she'd reveal. But she lifted her hand and went for her wrist. The twitch of her lips proved she knew exactly what she did to him. He squirmed on the wagon, again eager for her. Three buttons on her left wrist. Then she moved to her right.

"You putting on a show for Sy, Beth? Making him wait to see what you'll show?"

Her nostrils flared, but she said nothing. She tugged her shirt out of her skirt, flashing a bit of soft, white belly. He swallowed and shifted on the hard boards. Again, she almost undid her breast button. She sighed, then walked her fingers to the lowest button and started up. He rubbed his nose with his hand to hide his smile. The minx dared him to complain.

She was obedient, barely. She'd pay for putting him through this. And she'd enjoy every minute of it. Just as he enjoyed the torture she put him through now.

He untied his boots, tossed them aside, and hopped off the wagon. She watched him carefully remove his pants to reveal his cock, once again hard for her. His dark purple head already thrust out of its sheath, eager to slide between her legs, to brush past the tiny bud throbbing for release.

He stood tall, his third leg jutting proud. He caught a flash of light out of the corner of his eye. So Simon was hunting bee trees on this side of the ridge, against his orders. Normally Sy would make sure to guard against giving himself away but watching Beth undress would turn any man's mind from thoughts of safety.

Buttons finally undone, Beth flapped her blouse as if to create a breeze. She knew she waved a red flag at a bull. Her actions begged him to prove who was the boss. He'd show her who wore the pants in this family.

At the moment he was bare-assed but he'd put his pants back on after they played. She, however, would stay naked under her thin layer of protection. The only reason he let her wear her dress was to protect that fine skin from the sun. If they ever rode home in late afternoon, he'd make her ride beside him in nothing but her hat and boots.

Even better, she'd sit astride his lap, facing backward. Riding his cock, every bump would thrust him deep into her.

Enough!

He took a step toward her. The tip of her tongue stuck out between her teeth, just as her inner lips protruded from her outer.

"Shirt. Off."

"It's a blouse."

He took another step and the fabric fluttered to the grass.

"Skirt."

Nostrils flaring and chest heaving—damn, he loved her breasts—she undid the button at her waist. Her pretty skirt dropped, covering her boots. Her even prettier lower curls glowed in the sun, begging for his tongue.

His naked wife waited for him, nipples tight and eyes beckoning, on his land.

Bending slightly, he slid his cock straight forward into the open space between her thighs. He thrust slowly back and forth below her pussy. He rubbed his chest on her breasts, rasping the tips in the way he knew drove her wild. She fought it, but he felt her pussy swell around him. His cock slid more easily as her arousal increased.

Her glorious golden hair fell around them like a curtain. He ran his fingers through it, letting it fall over her shoulders. As he pumped, a flush rose, bit by bit, toward her face. He already knew her body. By the time it hit her hairline, she'd be ready for more. Time for another lesson.

"You're going to ride bareback today."

"Now?" Her blue eyes widened.

He nodded, still slowly pumping. He hadn't known he could come this often and still get hard, but he'd never had a wife before. Unlimited sex did things to a man. Great things.

"I thought that meant the horse didn't have a saddle, not that I'd be unclothed."

He liked her grit, sassing back at him while naked with his cock between her thighs.

"Don't need a horse."

"What are you after, Mr. Elliott?" She narrowed her eyes at him.

"This is what you'll ride."

He gripped her bottom, tilted and slid home. She gasped and clutched him, wrapping her legs around his waist. He waited for a moment of bliss, then pressed up until he'd skewered her well and good. He let them have a moment before pulling out and setting her down.

"Grab that wagon wheel."

He encouraged her to bend over and grasp the spokes near the wheel hub. He admired her ass, nice and round, then moved her feet farther apart.

"Arch your back and show Sy that sweet ass. Make him so hot that he comes in his pants just by watching you."

She glowered at him over her shoulder then did what he said. She wiggled, leaning forward and tilted her butt so her cheeks spread, showing him her brown dot. He'd ease her into that soon enough.

Below her asshole, thick pink lips swelled for him. He moved her slightly so the sun shone full on her, making her fluids glisten. He slid a finger to her clit and she moaned. He held himself in one hand, braced the other on her hip and guided himself in with a shallow thrust to whet his appetite. He bent over her back and held her breasts in his palms, enjoying their weight.

Without asking, Beth moved her thighs together, catching him tight. He pulled out before he exploded. Both of them panted hard.

"Time to ride," he said. He lifted her and carried her to the blanket he'd laid in a shady patch of grass when they first arrived. She'd thought they'd open Sophie's basket but his appetite was more carnal.

He knelt and set her down, then rolled onto his back, pulling her with him. He'd wanted that golden hair to tantalize his chest and cock since he first saw her.

"Ride me, woman."

Instead, Beth sank to her knees and grasped him hard. Smiling seductively, daring him to complain, she stroked him back and forth until he was full length, thick and wanting. She leaned forward and flicked the first drop off with her tongue. He hissed and almost came. He forced himself to do multiplication tables as she continued flicking his underside with her tongue.

God, she felt so good. He spread his legs wide so she had full access. She cupped him, sucking one ball into her mouth for a moment, then the other.

He concentrated on making it last, prolonging the joy for both of them. No way would he discourage her enthusiasm. She'd need it to keep up with three men. She caught him between her breasts. She reached down and gathered her own slickness, rubbing it over him to make him slide.

She finally released him and stood like a valkyrie tall above him. She tossed her golden hair back, shaking her head. It was so long it touched the crack of her ass. She stepped over him and sank down to her knees, one on each side of his hips. She leaned forward and sat back, guiding him in. She grasped him with greedy pussy lips, sucking him in, inch by inch, rising and falling in a molasses-slow canter. Her tight sheath enveloped him, the slow friction as frustrating as it was pleasurable.

"That's it, Beth. Show Sy what he's missing. Make it work, sweetheart."

He reached up to her breasts, quivering above him, and lightly pinched. She gasped, grinding down. He kept one hand on her breast and pressed the other where their flesh met, rubbing her mound. She moaned, mouth open and head back, slamming down on him. Finally, he felt her grasp him inside as she reached her peak.

He fought hard to stop himself from joining her as she met her own needs. A moment or two, then she twitched in place and leaned her fists against his chest, panting. Grinning.

"Your turn," she said.

He didn't wait. He grasped her waist and lifted. She followed his lead, slamming down as he pressed heels and shoulders into the ground and surged up. His need to prove to the world, on his own land, that she was his, added a bite. She caught his wave of pleasure and slipped into her own. His bellow and her cry of completion shattered the quiet.

* * * *

"What the—?"

Sitting tall on his gelding, Simon stared down at the trail from town. Was that dust raised by his fool of an older brother? When Trace still wasn't home for morning chores they figured the sheriff had tossed him in jail. Without big brother around to give orders, he headed up the wooded east face of the mountain to scout out a bee tree. It was too early in the season to remove honey so he marked the hive and started off home. Then he saw the plume of dust heading for Elliott land.

He pulled out his spyglass and followed the trail. He couldn't miss Trace's paint. The horse's large brown and white patches were unmistakable. It was tied behind a loaded wagon.

"Shit!" His horse skittered. He climbed off and tied it to a branch above long grass. "Dammit, it's *my* turn to go to town and get supplies!"

His horse looked up, ears perked. "I swear," he said to it, "if I had a shotgun loaded with rock salt I'd give him both barrels." He lifted the eyeglass again. "Let's see what big brother thought so all-fired important he had to haul it home today."

Simon found Trace's head, turned to one side. He watched Trace open his mouth and move his lips as if talking. Simon moved the glass to the side and saw a flash of pink.

"What the hell?"

He dropped to the ground and rested the spyglass on a rock for stability. His big brother sat next to someone in a pink bonnet. He watched as they pulled to a stop by the shaded stream to water the horses and stretch as usual. When it was warm the Elliotts always took a swim before the last leg home.

But Trace had something better in mind.

"Holy shit!"

Simon put down the glass, wiped his eye and looked back. When he found the pair again he focused on the golden beauty as she slowly stripped. He moaned as her full breasts emerged when she dropped her shirt. Soon her skirt followed it. Naked but for her boots, she watched Trace approach.

Simon clutched the spyglass. The three of them had a pact that, if any of them married and the woman was willing, she'd be shared.

"Please, God, let her be willing!"

Blondie grasped two spokes of the wagon wheel. "That's a fine ass," he murmured. "Smooth, pink and wide enough to grab onto."

She spread her legs and leaned over. Trace leaned close and slid into her from behind. He held her breasts as she arched to take him. But he pulled out after only a few thrusts. He carried Blondie to a blanket under the trees and lay down.

Simon's mouth went dry when she picked up Trace's cock and brought her mouth close. "Jesus! I didn't know decent women did that!"

He unbuttoned his pants and grasped his hard rod, imagining it was feminine flesh holding him tight. When he looked again, she rode Trace's cock, a smile like the angels on her face. And that hair!

Simon focused on the space between their bodies where they joined. She rose and fell, faster and faster. He followed her every move with his hand as if she rode him instead of Trace. She threw her head back, mouth open. Just after she screamed his brother's name Simon joined her for the best single-handed ride of his life.

Spent, he lay back on the grass, panting up at the sun and grinning like a fool.

"Way to go, big brother. You bring that wild angel home and we'll treat her right." He buttoned himself up and climbed on his horse. "Wait till Jackass finds what big brother's bringing home. I wonder if she can cook." The horse flicked an ear and ignored him. "Hell, lookin' like that, who cares if she can cook?"

Chapter Eight

Though Beth trembled inside, she kept her back straight as she sat beside Trace. As soon as Trace touched her naked body her mind went blank. Only as they ate the picnic Sophie had provided did she remember about Simon. Had he seen her naked, doing wicked things with Trace?

The parts so recently stimulated tingled once more at the thought. She was going to Hell, all right. No good woman got hot at the thought of her husband's brother seeing her naked. What would Simon do while he watched? Would he pretend he was the one she rode? Would he want her to do the same to him? Yes, Trace made that clear.

Would she want to? *Yes.*

She shivered in the hot sun. Though she could still feel her husband's hands on her, his body filling her, she wanted more. What had happened? Twenty-one years of denial gone in less than twenty-four hours. Was this need trapped within her all her life? Had it erupted from deep inside, unlocked by ecstasy?

Growing up, she'd never touched herself except to wash what had to be washed. Cold water and a rough cloth didn't invite one to linger. With many sisters, she'd never slept alone until she was sent to the farm. By the time she fell into her narrow cot, she was far too exhausted to do more than grab her few hours of sleep and start over again.

She'd escaped, taking the Bride Train all the way to Montana Territory. Trace had saved her from a terrible fate. Yet she sat beside him and actually considered sexual congress with his brother. Had this wickedness always been inside her, eager for any man?

No. She'd met many men since she left home, and none had made her feel like Trace. Would his brothers do the same? *Once you've bitten of the Apple, expulsion from Eden isn't far behind.*

"There's Jackass."

A man on a horse appeared from the woods as if he'd been waiting for them. Even from this distance she could see his body was almost as big as her husband's.

She grabbed the seat to steady herself at the rush of...was it trepidation or something more sinful? Trace was a very handsome man, at least to her. He turned her bones to jelly with one look. The man approaching set her quivering. How could she live in the same house with three of these men and not eventually give in?

"Where'd you find such a vision of beauty?"

Jack's voice, so melodious after Trace's harsh rasp, slid along her skin like silk. His hot smile, though aimed at her face, seemed to see her whole body at once. Unclothed.

Unbidden, her nipples rose. She felt a pull of attraction to this man. Not as strong as with Trace, but strong enough to send her to Hell.

She meant to button up her collar before they arrived but Jack caught her showing a hint of breast. She clenched her thighs at the rush of need that shot through her. How could this happen with her husband's brother, especially after she and Trace had just done wild things out in the open?

Trace lifted her onto his lap so she faced Jack. He caught and bunched up her skirt so her bare thighs rested on his rough pants.

That meant he could pat her bottom without his brother seeing. Trace grasped her thigh with his right hand. Jack tilted his head to look for Trace's missing hand. She gasped when Trace slid it under her skirt. Her bottom cheeks extended past Trace's knees, leaving her open to his hand. Jack's slow smile suggested he knew exactly what Trace did. She punched Trace in the shoulder. Both men laughed.

"Elizabeth, this is my brother Jack. Simon's his older twin. Jackass, this lovely creature is my wife, Beth."

"Good day, Mr. Elliott." Beth forced the words out, though she was almost breathless as Trace ran his rough hand over her bottom. She blinked in mortification and desire.

"Call me Jack, Beth. I can't *wait* to get to know you better." Jack lifted a finger to his hat in greeting and winked. "In addition to your obvious beauty, would you kno   w how to cook? Not that we'd mind if you couldn't. I could even choke down Trace's grub if I could see more of you." He waggled his eyebrows. "Lots more."

She hesitated, sure Trace would say something about Jack's bold comment. But he waited for her to answer.

"My husband hasn't asked about my cooking skills."

"Trace?" Jack hooted. "The man who lives by his stomach didn't find out before he married you?"

"There's more to a wife than food," growled Trace.

Beth felt him harden under her bottom as he continued to caress her. Face flaming, she reached behind and slapped his hand. The corner of Jack's mouth quirked up.

"Why didn't you invite your dear brothers to the wedding?"

"Had to get married last night."

Jack tilted his head and sucked his teeth for a moment.

"Had to? Where'd you find her?"

"Fighting Charlie in the hoosegow."

Jack lifted a dark eyebrow. "And why, pray tell, did our industrious sheriff lock milady away?"

"Beth fought back when Big Joe Sheldrake wanted to claim her. She gave him her knee and, while he was bending over, kicked him in the ass. Frank took her boots and locked her up for her own protection. If she'd had those boots on when I first saw her, Charlie'd still be screaming."

"I can protect myself!"

"You don't have to anymore," said Trace quietly. "The Elliott men will take care of you."

A silent signal shot from one brother to another but she couldn't decipher it.

"We surely will," said Jack. "Don't mind missing the wedding since you're bringing her home for the honeymoon." Jack wiped the sweat off his forehead and settled his hat back in place.

"Tell Sy there'll be four at supper," said Trace.

"Bet he already knows," replied Jack with a quick grin. His eyes sparkled along with the smile. As Trace said, he was a man for the ladies. "You know my twin. He went after a bee tree up there." Jack pointed to the north. "He'd see the wagon dust and check it out."

"Um, when would he have looked?" Beth held her breath.

"Soon's you got on Elliott land he'd have his spyglass out. Why?"

Beth's heart beat faster than when Trace's magic fingers caressed her. "When we stopped to water the horses you said we were on Elliott land," she whispered to Trace. "Do you think he saw us?"

"If you were doin' what I think you were, any red-blooded man would watch, ma'am!" Jack, with a wide, knowing smile, doffed his hat. He turned his horse and sped off, taking what must be a short-cut home.

"Huh," said Trace with an innocence she knew was false. "I told Simon not to go hunting a bee tree. Dang boy never did listen."

"Aren't you upset your brother might have seen us doing…that?"

Trace slid his right hand into her shirt using the gap between her neck and bosom. He brushed her hard nipples, causing her to shiver.

"Nope. The boy's seen naked women before. He'll get over it."

She arched her back when he kneaded her breast, her breathing erratic. "I don't care about that. Doesn't it bother you that another man saw me?" She was doomed. Jack had looked at her just like Trace did before he undressed her.

She fought back a moan when Trace moved his hand from her bottom to her front. He gently pressed her legs apart to reach her core. When he touched her like this she couldn't think, much less talk. She gave in to a moan, leaning back and spreading her knees while he stroked her. His nostrils flared and he grinned when he found the sweet spot between her legs soaking. She closed her eyes against his self-satisfied look.

"He's not another man, Beth. He's my brother." He sent two fingers into her, curling them forward against a wonderful spot.

"Why...*Oh yes!* Why is that different?"

"You'll be living with all of us. They're going to see you naked."

"What?" She forced her eyes open and stared up at him. His eyes were half closed, like a cat full of cream dozing by the fire. But the fire was in his touch.

"What if Simon saw you riding me?"

He lightly stroked her clit. She shivered and clenched her thighs, capturing his hand. He rasped a chuckle. She hadn't known this magical feeling existed when Trace protected her in the jail. Last night, this morning, and again by the stream, he'd shown her the rapture possible between a man and a woman. She craved his touch. But now she felt a pull to his brothers. She should be ashamed rather than eager.

"Thinking about Sy watching makes you wet, don't it? And you're wondering about Jack, too."

"Um..."

"Don't hide it, sweetheart. Your nipple was hard before I touched you."

Her mind whirled. What could she say? She knew wives were beaten for merely smiling in thanks when a man held the door. Trace leaned over and locked his dark eyes on to hers, holding her tight.

"Jack and Simon want you as much as I do, Beth. You're the only woman they've seen since before winter. We won't force you. But it isn't right if three brothers live in one house with a woman, and only one man gets pleasure." His lips rose in the sensual smile that melted her insides. "Especially if she can get pleasure from all of them."

She pressed her lips tight, refusing to understand his words. He gently brushed a knuckle over her cheek.

"If any other man touches you, he's dead. But we've shared everything since Ma and Pa died. Everything. You're an Elliott now. I want you to think about what that means."

Trace set her on the seat beside him. For the rest of the journey he watched the road, saying nothing. She twitched and fidgeted the whole way. Trace's straining pants told her how much he wanted her. His brothers would be the same. What if their touch made her as wild?

She'd exploded every time his hands, mouth, and manhood did those wonderful things to her. What would it be like to have three men bring her pleasure?

* * * *

Beth made sure every button was secure before the horses started up the last rise. Her new home was far bigger than the cabin Trace had mentioned, but she paid little attention. All she saw were the two big men waiting. As Trace said, Simon and Jack were not identical twins. Simon's hair was black and scruffy like Trace's while Jack's was brown and neat. Their clean-shaven faces, lighter where beards had stopped the sun, showed a few recent nicks.

"Welcome home, Mrs. Elliott. I'm Simon. You sure are pretty."

She could tell from Simon's knowing smile that he'd watched when they played. She burned wherever his eyes lingered. Trace lifted her down from the wagon. Her feet had barely touched down when he swooped her into his arms. He carried her into her new home and set her down facing the door.

"Time to kiss the new bride," said Jack, rubbing his hands and grinning.

"Later, boys," said Trace. "That wagon needs emptying."

When the three of them left she crossed her fingers. Having spent three days in jail while the local ne'er-do-wells dropped by, she could imagine what a house with three bachelors looked like. She turned around.

"Oh my!"

She stood in an open area facing stairs. The floor was dirty, of course, but far from the muddy mess she expected. Even better, it was made of wood and not pounded dirt. To her right was a kitchen with a long table and benches. On her left was a dusty parlor. Feeling as if she should tiptoe, she stepped down the narrow hall to the left of the stairs. Behind the parlor she found a room with a double bed, rocking chair, and dresser with mirror. Trace's bedroom, now hers as well?

None of the rooms had doors. She returned to the kitchen to find Simon placing the half-empty picnic basket on the recently scrubbed table.

"Me and Jack sleep upstairs," he said without looking at her. He went back out for another load.

That meant she'd share the doorless bedroom with her husband. Wouldn't a married couple have more privacy upstairs? But exploring could wait for more urgent matters. When she hurried out the door Trace pointed at the privy and she eagerly went to it. She almost cried when she discovered it also lacked a door. Worse, it had boards across the bottom. She had to lift her skirts high to step over. At least the open door faced away from the house. She wrinkled her nose at the smell, did her business quickly, and returned to the pump to wash her hands.

"We took off the door as soon as it warmed up since it gets a bit high in there after winter," said Jack, "but we can put it back on for you."

"It's hard to step over that barrier in skirts," she replied.

"Better than having a porcupine chaw away at the salt on the seat. That'll give you slivers in your ass." Jack's eyes lit up. "I'd be mighty proud to help get them out anytime you want."

She pretended she hadn't heard him. She followed the men into her new home. They placed fabrics and notions in the parlor and food in the kitchen. She stoked up the fire for a bracing cup of tea, then investigated the pantry. After the long winter many empty jars and stoneware crocks waited refilling, sitting upside down to keep vermin out. A few clear jars still held fruit, vegetables or sausages. She hoped there was potted meat in some of the crocks for a quick dinner.

"No work for you today," said Trace. He set down the last case of empty Mason jars. "It's Sy's turn to cook. You put your feet up while we finish the barn chores." He ushered her into the parlor. "I want you wide awake after supper. Tonight will be another first for us."

He left the room with a wink before his brothers caught them together. If Trace said to rest, she might as well take advantage of it. This might be the last time she'd be off duty.

She ran her finger though a thick layer of dust on a sturdy bookcase. Ewall's *Medical Companion* sat on the top shelf with Pike's *Arithmetic* and Byerly's *Speller*. A line of McGuffey's readers finished the row. The next shelf held her favorites, the collected works of Shakespeare. With six sons, the *Robinson Crusoe* and *Don Quixote* would be popular.

Trace's mother must have been a strong woman to raise all those boys and a daughter. She'd love to have seven children of her own. But there'd be laughter in her home, not the icy silence or furious fists she'd grown up with. She lifted a dust sheet off the horsehair sofa and settled back. She'd close her eyes for a moment, then make that cup of tea.

Nibbling lips roused her. She opened her eyes, relieved to discover her husband leaning over her. He held out his hand and helped her to her feet.

"The boys hung a curtain," he said, pointing to their bedroom. How had she slept through someone nailing up an old white sheet?

She followed Trace into the kitchen, wrinkling her nose at the smell of burned food. Jack and Simon stood up from the bench opposite her. The air disappeared from the room and her womanly parts melted.

All three men were ruggedly handsome, tall, dark, and broad. Trace's eyes were almost black, Simon's a gray-green and Jack's were brown. All three sets followed her every breath. She crossed her arms to hide her swollen nipples but fooled no one, as proved by their knowing smiles.

Trace could see how they looked at her, eager for her attention, but he said nothing. He held out the one chair for her. When she sat he leaned down. Holding her face with both hands, he kissed her. She knew he did it to brand her once more but she concentrated on his lips and their sensual caress. When he released her, he gently squeezed her breast. He strolled to the other end of the table and found his stool, leaving her gasping.

She dropped her burning face and stared at her clasped fingers, white with strain. Jack offered a platter of flat, black biscuits. The smell made her veer back. She shook her head.

"You burned the biscuits again, Sy," complained Jack. "They're so bad, the missus can't eat them."

It wasn't just the food. The tension around the table made her stomach clench. No matter how hungry, she couldn't force a bite down.

"I need to know if the golden angel Sy says has the bottom of Aphrodite, can cook," said Jack.

Beth glared at Simon who lifted his shoulders and held his hands out as if to say "how could I not tell him". She groaned, set her elbows on the table and dropped her head into her hands. He didn't say "body," but "bottom." He watched them, all right. The same heat that Trace created rose from below her belly.

"I asked about her cooking, but she wouldn't tell me," said Trace. He frowned at the black disk in his hand and banged it against the table. Not a flake chipped off. He spooned into his wooden bowl what must be stew. He offered the pot to her but she shook her head. Just the sight of it made her shudder.

Simon wrinkled his nose at the steaming bowl in front of him, then pushed it away. "When will she share her secrets with us?" he asked.

Reading more into the comment, Beth flicked her eyes to him.

All innocence, he smiled politely and turned to Trace. "Cooking secrets, I mean."

Trace shoved his bowl to the side. "Beth will share when she's ready."

She looked at her lap where her fingers knotted together as if she prayed. Trace already showed her more caring, affection, and respect than anyone had previously. He'd also shown her why a woman would work hard all day just to get the glory her husband provided at night. She looked up and caught his quick wink. He smiled behind his eyes, not to make a fool of her in front of his brothers but to show they were a team.

In their wedding vows, Trace promised to bed, breed, and care for her the best he could. Beth's fingers tightened, turning red and white from the pressure. She'd been so smug about not promising to obey Trace that she'd not thought about what she *had* promised. To take Trace into her bed and to care for him *and his family* and whatever children she produced. When he said there'd never be love, he also promised no Elliott would force her. She thought he meant cleaning stable muck off their boots or cooking prairie oysters when she couldn't even stand the look or feel of regular ones.

What man would share his wife with his brothers, without jealousy? No matter how far out in the wilderness, there were rules to be followed. Weren't there? She'd sworn never to have a marriage like her parents', with the man controlling every aspect of their life. Her father gave nothing but orders, and her mother meekly went along. Her father did everything to be accepted by the highest levels of society no matter the cost. Selling his eldest daughter to get out of a debt was nothing to dear Papa. He fit right in with his lying, cheating, brutal friends. They said one thing and did another. At least the Elliott men were honest about what they wanted.

Her.

Could she be honest with herself?

She liked what Trace did to her. More than that, she craved it. She couldn't imagine going through life without writhing under his fingers and tongue. The way he entered her so forcefully, face grimacing before he croaked his pleasure, made her eager to share marital relations.

Would the desire ever slow down? Simon stretched out his leg, his warm thigh rubbing against hers. An eager ache high between her thighs made her want to rub herself. Even better would be Trace's hard cock sliding into her.

What would Simon's feel like? She stared at his hand, watching his curled index finger glide up and down the handle of his carved spoon. Her mouth had slid over Trace's hot cock like that a few hours ago.

She reached for her water, letting her arm touch her breasts' hard tips as she moved. Like scratching a mosquito bite, it felt good for a moment, but she immediately wanted to do it again. Finally noticing the heavy silence, she lifted her eyes.

Three pair of eager eyes stared at her erect nipples. Three sets of nostrils flared whenever she inhaled. Her breasts tingled as the blood flowed into them. She clenched her inside muscles but it did nothing to ease her ache.

"Trace, I…"

He immediately stood behind her, his broad hands on her shoulders. "I didn't let you get much sleep last night, Beth. You need to rest for later."

She groaned inside. Why did he have to say that? Did he enjoy baiting his brothers? Both of them shifted as if their pants were too tight.

Trace drifted a finger over her cheek. "I have something for you. I think it will fit."

He kissed her temple and left the room. She looked at her lap so she wouldn't see the eager pleading eyes of his brothers. She heard a drawer open in the parlor. Papers rustled, and then it closed again. Trace took the few steps necessary from the parlor to the kitchen. He dropped to one knee at her left side. She looked down at his wide smile.

He brought his palm up and showed her the box sitting there. He opened it. A gold ring nestled on white satin.

"Beth, will you be my wife?"

She stared at the ring, then at her husband. Her gulp was loud in the room.

"I know the wedding wasn't what a woman dreams of. I'm not either. But this was my great-grandmother's ring. Will you wear it?"

She nodded, blinking to hold back tears. He took her left hand and slid the ring on her third finger. It was a bit loose but would fit once she gained back the weight she'd lost.

He stood up, leaned over, and took her face in his hands again. She closed her eyes to savor the light scratch of his moustache over soft lips on her cheek. His lips hardened, pressing hers open and entering her eager mouth. She burned for him, forgetting everything but her need for more. When he pulled away, she swayed, glad she was sitting down.

"You're so hot, Beth. Let me help you cool down."

He'd undone her buttons, all the way to the swell of her breasts, before she could stammer a refusal. He winked and slipped a rough hand over her breasts, chafing her nipple. She closed her eyes at the grins across the table and bit back a moan.

"I'll give you a cool sponge bath while the boys clean up."

"But…"

Hand under her elbow, he escorted her from the room. She tried to explain that she couldn't undress with two strangers in the next room and only a cloth for a door, but he wouldn't listen.

"They're not strangers, Beth. They're my brothers. You undressed for me on our wedding night."

"But you were my husband!" She hissed, trying to keep his busy hands from her buttons. No such luck. He had her down to boots in no time flat. Soon she was stark naked, and stark raving mad to have come here.

Until she met Trace, no man had ever looked at her as he did. His eyes devoured her, his need for her new but demanding. Her nipples crinkled hard under his gaze. He smiled, slow and sure, as her body instantly reacted.

He was her husband. He owned her. Every inch, inside and out. No matter that he made her flush with embarrassment, he wouldn't beat her. Instead, he gave her pleasure. If he wanted his brothers to help her scream her release, it was still far better than screaming in pain with Big Joe. She could do this. She could pretend she was married to them all.

But not yet!

"Wait here. I'll get some warm water and a cloth. No, I want to do this for you," he continued when she tried to protest.

She stood proud when Trace pulled aside the curtain. As expected, Simon happened to be standing where he could see her. He even had time for a saucy wink before the curtain fell. Her obstinate body reacted to him almost as it did with Trace, throbbing for fulfillment.

With Trace gone she could think. She crossed her arms and turned her back on them all. What they wanted, what she wanted, was a sin against the church. But then, what good had the church done her? They said it was God's will that women obey men in all things. She was to accept chastisement as her father or husband considered necessary, no matter how brutal. Her body belonged to her husband and her soul to God. She was only the vessel.

No.

Her body, mind, and soul belonged to herself. And she'd do what she wanted, when she wanted, how she wanted. And right now, she wanted some time to herself. Her husband, along with his handsome brothers, would have to live with it.

"Sy was right. Your bottom is like a juicy ripe peach."

She shrieked and whirled around, one hand up and one down to cover herself. Jack lounged against the doorway.

"Yep," he called over his shoulder. "You're right about the melons, too."

"Out of the way, Jackass. Beth's hot." Trace elbowed past, an enamel pan in his hands. The curtain fell into place behind him.

"Sure is," said Jack through the thin material. "But she ain't the only one."

Beth glared at her husband.

"Don't mind the twins," he said. "They wanted to see what a lucky man I am."

"You may never get lucky again, Trace Elliott."

"What's the matter, Beth?" The smile playing at the corner of his mouth sent her fury higher. His fingers unbuttoned his shirt. His wide chest, so comforting to lean against, appeared. She gulped.

"What's the matter?" she echoed. "Your two brothers just ogled me like, like, I was a basket of fruit! Don't you care that your brothers want to touch me?"

"Oh, I care, sweetheart," he rasped. He unbuttoned and kicked off his pants. Her eyes automatically dropped. She gulped as the source of her pleasure swelled. "I care so much it's killing me."

He stepped forward. She retreated until her back touched the bedpost. She grasped it behind her back to keep from reaching out to him.

"Know what's really making me want you?"

He slid his fingers through her damp curls. She shivered as he stroked her flesh, stoking her heat. Heart pounding, she watched his eyes darken.

"Knowing that my brothers seeing you naked makes you hot and wet." He leaned down to inhale the scent between her breasts. "Simon wants you," he said, kissing his way down her chest to her belly.

She clenched at every touch, knowing what he'd do when he

reached her core.

"Jackass wants you." He gently encouraged her to spread her feet apart with the backs of his hands. "And I want you. Now!"

He knelt between her wide legs, passed his arms between her thighs, and lifted her above his mouth. He hummed into her cunny, the vibrations spreading outward like a pebble in a pond. He shifted her sideways and pressed her bottom against the mattress. She lay back when he lifted her legs over his shoulders and, just as he had the first night, explored her.

He spread her pussy lips wide with two fingers, his eyes wide in wonder. He lightly trailed a finger along her inner lips. He followed that with his tongue.

She forgot about his brothers. About the curtained door. About everything but his magic tongue and fingers. She writhed on the bed, gasping and moaning, begging him for more until she crested.

He stood, held her hips with fingers damp from her release, and finally joined their flesh. She writhed, eyes closed, as he filled her need. Standing, he pumped, slow and steady, bringing her higher once more.

A greedy mouth engulfed her breast and she arched into it, reveling in the extra sensation. Trace's hands clenched her hips and plunged harder, faster. She gasped when a mouth captured her other breast and looked up. Three hungry pairs of eyes focused on her. Someone tweaked her clit and she exploded, Trace's roar barely registering over the blood rushing through her ears.

Chapter Nine

"I will kill him," she muttered. "Slice off body parts and stew them. Starting with the sausage between his legs. Then I'll start on his brothers."

Beth faced the wall, curled on her side with the covers clenched tight. How dare his brothers touch her without an invitation! No matter how wonderful it felt, she wanted control. It was *her* body they'd pleasured!

"No you won't, sweetheart," growled the voice that sent her anger, and libido, soaring.

"Why not?" Her growl was almost as gruff as his.

Trace lay down behind her, spooning on top of the sheet. He slid his hand over her breast and pulled her to him. "Because you like the idea of sharing with us."

"It's wrong!"

"Says who?"

"The Bible! Thou shalt not covet thy neighbor's wife!"

"We would never do that."

She shoved his hand away and tilted her head to look at him. He lazed on his side, chin on one fist, the other now fingering her hair. His organ was hard. Again.

"Yes, you would. Simon and Jack covet your wife. Me!"

"They're not neighbors."

"You know what I mean!"

He pulled her close. No matter how much she struggled to escape, he was too strong. She couldn't move with his arm holding her chest, his leg holding both hers down.

"Beth, we Elliott boys have been together all our lives. When Ma and Pa died, I was sixteen, already a man. My five brothers and sister were between nine and fourteen. The MacDougals took in the youngest four and they helped as they could, but they moved to Texas to get away from the miners. Me, Jack, and Simon kept the ranch going and each other alive by sharing what we had. There's nothing I wouldn't give my brothers. Nothing."

"That doesn't mean *I* want to give them anything!"

He kissed her nose as if she were a kitten. She tried to bite him, but he growled a laugh and pulled back.

"I said this before—we wouldn't make you do anything you didn't really want to."

She glared.

"Yes, I'll push a bit, but if you said no, I'd stop." He drew circles over her breast with his finger, right around her areola. She slapped a hand over his to stop him. "Remember when we played near the wagon? You thought someone watched, didn't you?" She hesitantly nodded. "Thinking one of my brothers might watch, didn't you perform a little? Throw your head back and lift those breasts high when you rode me?"

Heat rushed up her belly in memory, but she didn't answer him with words.

"Simon and Jack are in the barn, hard and horny after helping to pleasure you. They'll spend the night there, but I doubt either of them sleeps. They don't want to embarrass you." He choked back a laugh. "Okay, more than they already have." He grew serious. "They're men, Beth. Grown men with a man's needs. Not only are you the only woman available, you're beautiful. Of course they want you!"

She muttered, "Thanks a lot," not meaning it.

"That you're so hot and eager, so smart and feisty, only makes us want you more, Mrs. Elliott."

She inhaled a deep breath and then sighed it out. Why get angry when he praised her for the very things her parents hated?

"What are you going to do with me?"

"Right now? I'm going to hold my wife in my arms until we both feel better. Then I'll make you a cup of tea."

She sighed and relaxed. No matter how angry, she felt wanted in his arms. Safe. It meant so much after a lifetime of knowing no one wanted her.

"And after?" He rolled her to her back. He nuzzled her cheeks, then lips, slowly and sensuously. He rolled his tongue under her upper lip the way that drove her wild. He nibbled her earlobe and then kissed her until she half-melted. "What happens after is up to you," he panted.

She looked up at him for a few minutes while he brushed her hair back from her face.

"What's wrong, sweetheart?"

"I'm frightened."

She tried to stop her lower lip from quivering but couldn't. Neither could she stop tears from leaking. They slid toward her ears like molten lava, branding her as a coward.

"We'll protect you. Big Joe can't touch you here." He licked them up, following their path with sensual kisses.

"That's not it. I know you'll protect me." She ran her fingers through Trace's chest hair. "It's just that...oh, I don't know."

"Is it Simon? He's a big man, almost as big as me. Ugly as sin, but he's my brother so what can I do?" He shrugged, jiggling her a bit as the bed bounced. "Does Simon scare you?"

She pulled her lips in, fighting a smile since both men looked so much alike. She shook her head.

"If not Simon, it must be Jackass. He's a smooth-tongued devil. Loves flirting with the ladies but he's too bashful to do much about it. Does he scare you?"

Again, she shook her head.

He sighed heavily and looked away. "It's me, then. My ugly voice scares the hell out of most people, why should you be any different?"

"You don't scare me. I think you're a wonderful man."

"Then who're you afraid of?"

"Me."

"Why?" He settled behind her, holding her close. She bit her lip, fighting tears.

"You can tell me anything, Beth. I'll never leave you."

"What if I fall in love with all of you?"

"Love?" His heart, behind her shoulder, pounded so fast she thought she might get a bruise.

"I know you won't ever love me, but I accept that. To my parents, I was a something to use. When I refused their orders, they threw me out. I've only known you a few days, but I've never loved anyone like I do you. What if I lose you...will Simon and Jack care for me? What if they find wives and bring them back here? Then what happens to me?"

"You..." He cleared his throat. "You love me?"

"Why else would I want to be with a man who makes me so mad I could just spit, yet I want him to strip me naked and take me right now, hard and fast?"

His heart sped up another thousand beats a minute, pounding against her.

"Sweetheart, you get me so riled up I don't know whether to spank your sweet bottom or thrust so deep you can barely breathe."

"You try to spank me, Trace Elliott, and I'll make sure every biscuit you eat is burned to a crisp!"

"I told you never to challenge me, wife." A slow smile spread over his face, lighting even his eyes.

"Or what?" she demanded.

* * * *

Beth shrieked when Trace flipped her belly onto his thighs. He ran his palm over her back, up and over her luscious bottom. The vixen fought him, trying to push up. This is what he wanted in a woman. Fire and passion. He grinned like a fool, already hard for her once more. He used his right ankle to hold down her legs, his left hand on her back. She bucked, thrusting her sweet bottom high. Her womanish talk of love scared the hell out of him, but this he could handle.

She squealed when the flat of his palm hit her flesh with a loud smack. She struggled as he watched his handprint turn white, then a rosy pink. She raged, fighting hard to escape. He gave her a smack to match on her other cheek, causing another squeal. He released her legs enough to insinuate a finger between her thighs.

As he expected, she didn't try to escape. Plunging deep, he brought tell-tale moisture up her crack. "Fight me as hard as you like, woman. I'm the one in charge."

"You better sleep with one eye open for the rest of your life." She screamed her words, kicking her feet up and down.

Another smack and she jerked. He inhaled her nectar, evidence of what she really wanted. He drew her freely flowing juices back and pressed against her asshole. The top of his finger easily breached her and she shivered. He could tell she'd fought to hold back the moan that escaped.

"That's it. Take me deeper."

He released her legs in order to spread them farther apart. He added a second finger to his backside exploration. He pulsed his fingers in and out while spreading them apart to widen her opening. She mewed a complaint when he pulled out. He flipped pillows under her belly and set her atop them, legs wide and bottom high. He gave her one last love tap and she quivered under him.

"Don't move!"

He strode to the kitchen, smeared a few fingerfuls of lard on a plate, and returned. She hadn't moved. Her rear end faced him, back arched to thrust her white cheeks high, each marked with his hand. Her pussy and bottom glistened with moisture. She panted hard, as did he.

He spread some lard on her hole. His finger slid in so easily. She moaned. He took his time to stretch her. More lard, then an additional finger. When she was eagerly pushing against all four fingers, he took position behind her.

His beautiful, smart wife knelt before him, offering herself to him, to do as he pleased. As they pleased.

Her golden hair clouded the bed, her smooth back rising to deep back dimples above plump buttocks. From here, he could see her swollen pussy weeping for him, clenching to pull his cock deep inside her.

He nibbled the patch of dark freckles on her left butt cheek. They almost looked like a ring. He kissed his handprints, still pink against her paler flesh.

When he took her virginity, though she was eager, she'd been tight. He was the first man she'd taken in her mouth and she'd enjoyed it. And now, he'd be the first to take her ass.

Only when he'd been her eager first all three ways, would he share her.

"Tell me if you're not okay. This may hurt, Beth. Tell me to stop if you need to." He smeared lard over the swollen purple head of his cock, rested it against her tiny hole and pressed. She relaxed and her tight pink ring expanded, opening to him. Damn, he wanted to see his thick cock disappear between her ass cheeks, hearing her moan in pleasure as she took him this way.

"I see a ring of pink, Beth. That means you're ready for me. Push me out," he said. "It will open that sweet hole and let me enter you easier."

He placed both hands on her cheeks and forced them apart. Stretching her wide like this would make it easier for her to take him. Suddenly his wide purple head popped through her tight ring of muscle. As when he'd broken her maidenhead, he stopped and let her adjust to him. Though he'd done little to build up a sweat he felt like he'd spent the day hauling logs.

"How is it?"

"Mmm. More," she murmured.

Inch by slow inch, he eased himself into her. This first time, he went in only half way. Holding himself in his fist to limit his depth, he worked in a slow rhythm, quivering one hand on her pussy.

She was so hot. So tight. So needy. He fought the incoming wave of orgasm with everything he had. Her trust in him finally overwhelmed him.

"I can't last, I..." He pulled almost out, then back in, unable to release her. He caught her clit between his fingers and squeezed.

"Oh, yes. Yes!"

Beth's scream of release brought his own. Pumping fast but shallow, he extended their pleasure until they fell to their sides, still together.

Chapter Ten

Simon set his shovel down and wiped the sweat off his forehead with his dirty right sleeve. Jack spotted him and headed over from the corral.

"We don't need a new shitter, Sy. There's still some room left in the old one." Jack leaned over to inspect the freshly-dug trench. "I came home early to put the door back on for Beth." Acting as a self-appointed supervisor, he pointed to a corner that wasn't quite square.

"Don't want a door," replied Simon. "It'll stink worse than an old miner leaving his cabin after a three-week blizzard." He set his fists on his hips and stretched out his back. "I'm digging this one just for Beth."

All day while Simon worked he thought about Beth's reaction to the surprise. How she'd rub liniment on his sore muscles after supper. Though he ached from nose to toes, the part swelling against the buttons below his waist needed her touch the most.

"If you'd told me, I might've stuck around to help." The toe of Jack's boot nudged the dirt pile so that a clump fell into the hole. Simon pretended he didn't notice, part of their unending game.

All six Elliott boys resembled each other physically. Their personalities were different but all were hell-raisers. At least, they had been the last time Simon saw them, seven years earlier. Back then Jessamine, thirteen and next in line after Jack, still had the Elliott stubbornness. Since there was no word of her settling down with a husband, Simon doubted she'd changed much.

"Couldn't say anything at breakfast with Beth right there, then you grabbed the last of her buttermilk biscuits and lit out. By the time I finished my coffee, you were gone."

"Eating those biscuits made riding a little more tolerable." Jack cupped himself, wincing.

"That's why I spent the morning digging this trench wearing these loose old pants."

"Better you than me," taunted Jack.

"But I was near in case Beth needed help with her bath."

"A bath?" Jack swallowed hard. "You see anything?"

Simon lifted his shovel and went back to work, ignoring Jack's mutters and letting the silence stretch. He had far more patience than the man three minutes younger. He tossed a shovel's worth of dirt and rocks on Jack's boots.

"Dammit, Sy. Tell me!"

"I get your next helping of dessert." Simon waited for Jack's jerked nod of agreement. "Beth didn't have a bath, but she scrubbed the floor after dinner. She said she needed a strong man to dump the bucket." He set the shovel on the ground and climbed out. He used his one inch height advantage to look down on Jack. "Better take your boots off before going inside or you won't get supper."

"Huh, I gave up my dessert and you tell me you saw nothing." Jack crossed his arms over his chest, emphasizing his extra muscle.

"I never said that."

Jack dropped his arms, made fists, and stepped closer. "What the hell? You want your nose rearranged again?"

As an Elliott, Simon never backed away from anything, especially with a brother. Sometimes a good fight was just what they needed to clear the air. Women didn't understand that, so he answered Jack rather than start something that would make Beth angry and wreck all the good will he'd spent the day creating.

"The floor was so dirty she had to slosh water over it. Her dress got all wet, and she had nothing underneath."

"Hot damn, and all I got was a couple extra biscuits." Jack slammed his right fist against his left palm. "I'm going to fill up the water reservoir on the stove so she can have a bath tonight."

"Already did that." Simon lifted a challenging eyebrow.

"Then I'll chop some kindling so she can light the stove." Jack stepped closer to Simon.

"Done that, too."

"You leave me anything to impress her?"

"Yep, something that suits you perfectly. Spreading lime and ash down the hole to kill the stink. Not that you'd notice it."

"For that, I'm gonna clean your plow. Again."

Simon snorted in disbelief as Jack started unbuttoning his shirt. Ma always whupped them for the extra work it caused her to repair the damage so they'd learned early to take their shirts off before they went at it.

"Funny, I remember it the other way around."

Women didn't understand that when he couldn't take her to bed, the next best thing was a free-for-all.

"You jackass, fighting would get Beth so mad she might refuse to serve supper. I'm not gonna chance it."

Jack scowled and stopped with his shirt half way undone.

"How long you think before she gives herself to all of us?"

"It's already too long," muttered Simon.

"I got an idea." Jack moved closer and dropped his voice. "What if we tease her, get her all riled up, stop just short of her release then do it over again? If she's as frustrated as us she'll give in pretty damn quick."

"You going to tell the brand-new bridegroom that?"

"Tell me what?"

Simon reached for the pistol he'd left upstairs before he recognized Trace's croak. Letting someone sneak up on him proved what thinking about a woman did to a man's survival skills.

Trace took a good look at the trench before turning to Simon. "You think building Beth her own privy will make her haul you into bed?"

"Nope, but Jack thinks keeping her on the edge will encourage a quick and enjoyable decision," explained Simon.

Trace screwed up his face. "Hell, no! Not if I have to go without."

"Dammit, man, we're hurting something awful!" Jack grimaced and pulled at the tent in his rough canvas pants.

"So am I and it's only been since this morning," replied Trace.

"Dang it man, don't boast about it to us!"

"Yeah, and if we go without, so can you. Got it?" Jack jammed his trigger finger against Trace's chest.

The clang-clang-clang of a triangle called them to supper. Trace waved his hat at Beth, standing on the porch up the hill from them. She waved back with her arm and went inside.

"I'll think on it while we eat. Simon, change your shirt before you sit at Beth's table. Jack, do yours up."

* * * *

Jack contemplated stripping and jumping in the creek to cool his swollen cock, but he was too hungry to take the time. The relief would only be temporary as one look at Beth and he'd be just as hard again. He pushed it out of his mind and concentrated on his stomach rather than parts south as he washed his hands and face beside his brothers.

Over the years they'd shared everything, even the painful need for release. But unless something happened, tonight Trace would take Beth to bed, again. He'd have to lie in the barn and listen to Beth's orgasmic screams. He'd grip his cock along with her cries of release then grit his teeth and try to sleep.

All three of them shucked their boots at the open door and hung their hats on pegs. Jack moaned just as loud as the others when he inhaled the savory aroma drifting past his nose.

"I lost track of time cleaning so it's only beans and bacon for supper," said Beth. She lifted her chin as if unsure of their reaction but determined to follow through anyway.

"Smells mighty good," said Trace. He glared over his shoulder, sending a silent, unnecessary message. Considering the barely edible grub they'd put up with for years, neither he nor Simon would dare to say a word of complaint.

Jack stood beside Simon at the bench and waited as Trace seated Beth. Knowing his brothers were hurting, Trace still nibbled Beth's ear, dang it! She flushed and crossed her arms but not before Jack saw two bumps rising from her chest.

Last night he'd taken the left one in his mouth, savoring it like a starving man. He could still taste her skin, could feel the way she stiffened under his hands when she gasped and went rigid. Someday, God let it be soon, he would be the one pumping into her while she screamed his name.

"You hungry or not?" An elbow in his ribs knocked him back to reality. He automatically struck out with his right hand, punching Simon in the upper arm. Something whacked him on his left knuckles. He whipped his head around to find Beth glaring at him, serving spoon covered in beans raised high.

"No fisticuffs in my kitchen!"

"Yes, ma'am." Jack licked the beans off his knuckles and kicked Simon under the table. He winced when his bootless foot caught the sturdy wooden table leg instead. Simon snickered but Jack was so hungry for decent food that he ignored his twin and dug in. There'd be time later for payback.

Beth had added onion and some sort of greens to the beans and bacon and turned it into something like he'd find in Sophie's dining room in town. He took longer eating the second bowl. Even the cornbread, something so quick and easy even he could cook it, tasted far better thanks to Beth. He wiped out his bowl with the last of the cornbread and sighed. If his cock wasn't happy, at least his belly was.

"Since Beth made dinner we've got an extra hour before evening chores," said Simon. "We could cover the trench with those warped boards we took off the barn."

"Simon decided you needed your own privy," said Trace to Beth as she picked up Simon's empty bowl. She smiled like a blonde angel. Trace shoved his bench back and stood. "You can thank him later. We'd better get to it while there's still light."

For once Jack was glad he was the youngest and always had to go last. He carried his bowl and coffee mug to the pile of dishes, which happened to be near Beth.

"Thank you for a wonderful meal, Mrs. Elliott." He placed a hand lightly on her waist and kissed her forehead. He breathed in her scent, torturing himself, then walked out and quietly shut the door. He was so hard it hurt to bend over and tie his boots but the stolen kiss was worth it.

* * * *

"We should be able to finish the job tomorrow," said Trace to Beth as he dried his hands on the towel she held. "I have to ride up to the ridge in the morning, but we've got enough boards cut that Sy and Jack can at least put up a few walls."

"Four walls, a roof and a door," she corrected. Beth figured this was the only privy they'd build her so she'd better put her demands front and center before they started taking her for granted.

"Yes, ma'am," said Simon. Jack, shoulder against the wall opposite his twin, nodded in agreement.

Beth tugged to get her towel back but Trace held tight, wiggling his eyebrows at her. She knew what that look meant and didn't want Trace to start anything until they were alone. She released the towel. Trace flipped it around her waist and pulled them close together.

"It'll cost you, wife," he said.

"One of my gold coins should be more than enough." Beth pushed back on his chest with her palms but he just smiled down at her, unmoving.

"Your gold's no good. Right, boys?" Trace released the towel, cupping her bottom to hold her against him.

When he began massaging her cheeks through her skirt she raised herself on her toes and tilted her hips, replying to his eager message. Jack shuffled his feet, startling and reminding her they were watching.

"Time for bed," growled Trace.

Beth shivered. When he used that tone she knew he could barely hold himself back. She was the same, having been taunted all day by wicked thoughts. She knew Simon watched her bottom when he passed the open door as she scrubbed the floor on her hands and knees. It was hot work and she didn't mind when a bit of rinse water splashed on her face. It felt so good she dampened her gown.

When she called Simon to empty the heavy bucket for her his eyes had caressed her breasts though the near-transparent material. They hardened at the attention, just as they did now.

"Simon, Jack, come say good night to Beth."

Trace released her, then turned her to face the twins. She looked from one, to the other. They stared at her as if she was the only morsel of food in the wilderness and they'd gone without for weeks.

"Who's first?"

Jack swaggered over as if daring Trace to change his mind. He stopped in front of her. "Thankee for the supper, ma'am."

"You're welcome, Jack."

She tilted her head so he could kiss her temple. But he slid his arms around her waist pulling her to him as Trace had done. Once more she felt the hard ridge of a cock pressing into her belly.

She gasped, and that's when he dropped his head to caress the side of her neck. With no moustache to tickle, she relaxed and enjoyed Jack's nibbles. He traced a path to her throat. She tilted her head back, leaning it on Trace's chest.

Jack's hands moved up her ribs, his thumbs making small circles as he kissed her throat. He brought his hands forward and brushed her breasts as if by accident. She twitched. Trace reached from behind and covered them with his own hands.

"I guess that's good night, Beth," said Jack. He pecked her cheek and moved away. Trace moved his hands to her hips.

"My turn," said Simon.

He stepped close and she automatically looked up. His eyes were more gray than green like an approaching storm.

"Remember me, the man who spent all day digging and carrying buckets for you? I certainly remember these, pointing to me through your wet dress." He brushed the tips of her hard nipples, aroused from Trace's touch, with the backs of his knuckles.

"Simon needs a reward for all that hard work," whispered Trace in her ear.

* * * *

Simon looked down at the wide-eyed aroused woman before him. He didn't have to look far, as the top of her golden head reached his nose. He inhaled a touch of roses as well as hard soap, onions and bacon. Rose-scented soap? The next time he went to town he'd make sure to buy a cake or two for her. He'd save it for the time it was *his* hands cupping her soapy body.

Starting at her nose, he laid a series of kisses across her cheek to her ear. Each slow and separate, he added the little bit of practical experience with what he'd heard.

He'd played checkers one night with Sukie, one of Miss Lily's girls, using shot glasses instead of markers. Half way through the game Sukie began telling him how to make a woman want you no matter what. He'd slowed his moves, losing a few extra markers to learn what drove an experienced woman crazy.

He'd never had the opportunity to try it out before, but from Beth's murmurs, she enjoyed it so far.

From her ear he curled around her jaw to her mouth. He pressed his tongue along the seam of her lips. When she opened for him he caressed her chin then held her head gently in his palms. He slid his tongue in front of her teeth under her upper lip, slow and sensuous, as if nothing else existed in the world except her.

Beth flicked her own tongue against the underside of his. Since she wanted to take an active role, he let her lead the dance. Their kisses deepened when Beth reached around and pulled him to her. When she broke off to breathe, he backed away though every part of him fought to push forward.

But Sukie said to make sure he was the one to stop. That way the woman was not quite satisfied and would want more. Sukie insisted the final reward would be worth it. With no one else to guide him, Simon followed her suggestions to the letter.

Three days ago, he'd worked long hours with nothing to look forward to at the end of the day other than lousy food followed by a lumpy mattress beside his snoring, farting twin. He had no reason to believe that life would change.

Then he looked through his spyglass and saw Beth strip and bend over the wagon wheel far below. The three of them had often gone months without a woman. Working to exhaustion all day lowered the need since they crashed into bed only to haul themselves up again a few short hours later. It was far different with a woman around to remind them of what could be.

But he would be patient if it killed him, and tonight it damn well might.

"Good night, Beth," he said. He pressed a kiss on her forehead, nodded at Trace and followed Jack across the dark yard to the barn.

Chapter Eleven

Trace floated in a wonderful place. Fresh, fragrant coffee drifted past his nose. An aroma of apple pie set his mouth salivating. Someone called his name, but he didn't want to leave this place of pleasure.

A hand crept under the covers. It stroked his cock, stirring him to life.

"Rise and shine. If you don't hit the table in three minutes, your brothers will have finished all the apple tarts."

His feet hit the floor before his brain engaged. He managed to avoid tripping on the sheet but had to grab the wall to stay upright. Light feminine laughter rewarded his performance.

He cracked his eyes open and discovered he faced the wrong way. He blinked at the bright sunlight streaming in the clean window. A sharp smack on his ass made him whirl around. Beth spun away, wooden spoon in hand and delight dancing in her eyes.

"Your brothers have eaten almost everything, sleepyhead." She danced out of the room.

"What?" he roared. How had he slept in? He never slept in!

He threw aside the bedroom curtain and strode into the kitchen, stopping when he saw Simon and Jack sipping coffee before a plate of pastries. At breakfast the previous day he'd stared at crisp, not burned bacon, perfect eggs, and lump-less porridge. But today a delightful odor of apple and cinnamon wafted past his nose.

"*Your wife* said we couldn't eat until you sat down to breakfast," groused Simon.

"So sit your hairy ass in the chair," ordered Jack.

He glared from one to the other. Soft hands snaked around him and captured his morning glory. Jack must have had the right idea. He'd gotten Beth so hot and bothered last night that she'd pounded on his chest, demanding satisfaction. He'd refused and spent the night cursing. If a wonderful breakfast and horny wife was the result, one frustrating night was worth it.

"You have to kiss the cook before you can eat, big boy," said Beth, laughing.

He looked at the food, then over his shoulder at his wife.

"No one can eat until I sit down?"

"Those are the rules," she said. "Husbands have a few privileges."

He turned to face her, cock rampant. She'd already learned what that look meant. "Trace?" she said, gulping.

"I'm going to kiss the cook all right. But not on those lips."

"But…"

"You woke the tiger, sweetheart. Now you pay the price."

He'd taught her that running away only made her "punishment" last longer. He'd take her close to fulfillment with his mouth and fingers, again and again, until she begged him to let her release. If she thought last night was going to make her crazy, today would send her to Bedlam.

He slowly unbuttoned the front of her dress. A blush rose to her face, though her nipples were hard. When he reached her hips, he pushed the fabric over her shoulders and it dropped to her feet. As ordered, she was naked underneath.

Simon and Jack, facing them, twitched on their bench, teeth gritted and fists on the table. Hands on her waist, Trace stepped forward, making her step back. Realizing his plan, Jack and Simon cleared the table, not bothering to sit again. Trace lifted his wife, placed her bottom on the table so her knees touched the edge, and stepped back.

* * * *

Beth, shivering in the morning chill, looked around. The faces of all three men were set in determined lines. Trace sometimes looked like that when he entered her, face screwed up as if in pain. His cock bounced gently in time with the raised vein on his temple. Sunlight caught the diamond drop quivering on his tip. She licked her lips, knowing how good he tasted.

She inhaled when he slid his finger into her cleft. She'd gotten up early to surprise him. When Simon and Jack came in, they quietly sat and watched her. They knew she wore nothing under her dress but her skin. Did they know how Trace had teased her, then refused her pleas? Their obvious hunger for far more than breakfast had her rubbing her wet thighs when she walked. If Trace wouldn't give her what she needed today, Simon and Jack looked eager to ease her ache.

Trace leaned over and nibbled her breast. She arched into him. He stepped between her thighs and settled her bottom at the edge of the table. The contrast between her hot flesh and the chilly wood made her gasp. He surged into her and she moaned, encouraging his deep thrusts. Her need rose, but before she crested he shuddered, exploding into her.

"That's not fair, you did that last night!" she cried. She leaned back on her hands, legs dangling. He stood tall and proud, panted and grinning like a fox. She tingled where he'd entered her, twitching for more.

Trace gently pressed until she lay on the table. He set her heels on the edge and backed away. "Boys, show the lady what you can do for her. Unless you've got a problem with that, wife? If you don't want them to touch you, it'll be a while before I get hard again. You'll be frustrated until tonight or tomorrow. Just like Simon and Jack have been since snow fell. You want me to help you to your feet?"

Beth flushed. The men had felt this need that drove her crazy for that long? They'd watched her walk around with hard nipples, having only had a taste, yet had never tried to force her?

Her breasts tingled along with the button between her legs. If they had that much self-control, she could trust them with every part of her life. This was it. She was ready to do with another man what she'd been taught was only for her husband.

Aching for release, she shook her head. "I want more."

"Obliged," said Jack.

He stared at her body like a starving man. Nostrils flaring, he stripped as if his pants were full of red ants. His thick cock throbbed, bouncing up and down with each heartbeat.

He knelt on the floor between her legs and trailed his fingers over her petals with a light, frustrating touch. She writhed, needing more. He stood, eyes wide and mouth grimacing, and guided his cock into her, hissing as if her channel burned him.

He pressed forward, stretching her in a most wonderful way. She met Trace's eyes. Not angry, but proud. She watched her husband as his brother thrust deep into her. She wrapped her legs around the man, determined to keep him until her need was met. But Jack exploded within seconds, heaving as if he'd outrun a bear. She gasped with need, still unfulfilled, and released him.

"My turn, I believe," said Simon. Jack pulled out and leaned against the wall, gasping for air and grinning like a wolf.

"You'd better take care of me first, or I'll never bake anything sweet again!"

"I'll always take care of you, Beth," he replied. He plucked her nipples, raising her heat before sliding in. He was longer but narrower than Trace. He bent and angled up inside her, sliding against something wonderful. She clenched him in surprise and delight. Trace grasped a breast and kissed her nipple. Simon continued to rub against her spot. He fingered her lips and teased her clit. She closed her eyes, arms flat on the table as she writhed.

Both breasts were engulfed in hot mouths, their teeth lightly rasping. She groaned as Simon stretched her. He drove her need even higher when he held her hips and pounded hard. She lifted her hips to meet each thrust, just as eager.

"That's it, Beth," growled Trace. "Let go. You deserve your reward."

Simon rubbed her clit just so and she exploded. Simon prolonged her release, pumping a few more times before roaring in triumph.

* * * *

"Remember the time Pa caught you in the barn with the peddler's old maid daughter? You musta been fifteen." Simon dished himself more potatoes.

All three men arrived for supper that evening still wet from the creek, boasting about which of them half-drowned the others. Their high spirits and one-upmanship continued all during the meal.

"Yep," replied Trace. "Blistered my butt so bad I ate standing up for weeks."

"Yeah, but did he catch you before or after?"

"Just starting round three. She was a demanding gal. "

The three men laughed. After working all day scrubbing clothes and floors, cooking and gardening, Beth still wasn't sure what she thought about that morning's craziness.

At least the tension that had strained every moment was gone. She'd taken a quick sponge bath in the kitchen but couldn't forget the feeling of each man coming in her. Would they expect the same thing now? She had enough work to do without taking care of the "personal needs" of three men.

"Simon, now that the road's dry, you'd better return the wagon," said Trace. "Tomorrow, first thing."

"I'll follow with ours," said Jack.

Trace frowned at him. "Why take our wagon into town?"

"I expect Beth has a few things to buy now she's seen what's missing."

Beth looked at Trace. Would he trust her to go to town with his brothers? Or should she say, did he trust his brothers with her?

"You need things, Beth?"

"Seeds for the garden, more preserving jars. A few more pie plates would be good since you men seem to think you need one pie each. And I'd like to mail a letter—"

"All right, we'll all go to town in the morning. There might be a letter from Texas. I forgot to check, with the wedding and all."

"You mean the bedding," said Simon, winking at Beth.

She blushed and looked down. The heat she felt had something to do with her time over the hot stove, but not much.

"The Elliott boys ride again!" Jack's wide smile showed what he used to charm the ladies.

"I'd like to thank Miss Lily for the lovely nightgown," said Beth. "Would I be allowed to do that?"

"With three of us escorting you, no one would dare touch you," said Trace.

"But, would it ruin me in the eyes of the ladies of the town? I'm going to be living here the rest of my life, and if I'm not accepted..."

"Trace said you spent three days in jail, barefoot, ogled by damn near every man in town," drawled Jack. "Big Joe wanted to marry you in the saloon, but a half-drunk Preacher read the good book over you in the jail." He sucked his teeth like an old miner. "Darlin', you were ruined even before you slept in the same house with two horny bachelors."

"Nothing happened between us!" Their guffaws raised her ire. "Not until this morning. And no one would know anything about that!"

Trace lifted her hand and kissed her knuckles.

"Sweetheart, if Jack and Simon don't spend the day holed up at Lily's, they'll know."

She opened her mouth, thought about it, then groaned. If they bedded Lily's girls, no matter how clean, she wouldn't want them to touch her. But if they didn't, she'd be labeled "no better than she should be." Either way, she was ruined. The spinsters, jealous widows, and haughty wives would attack her. Not that she wanted anything to do with them.

"If you smile like you did this morning, damn near every man will wish he'd been the one to offer for you. Even the married ones," said Jack.

"The women will be jealous you've got three strong men to pamper you," said Simon.

"Pamper?" she replied, setting her fork on her empty plate. "I spend the day working my fingers to the bone, and you think I've been pampered? Listen here, you—"

Before she could finish the sentence Trace tilted back her chair and captured her mouth. After the session that morning, instead of being fulfilled, she wanted more. All day, her pussy lips rubbed against each other as she worked. The cool bath hadn't helped. His kiss engulfed her, his tongue plundering her mouth as she wanted him to do elsewhere.

Someone scooped her up and Trace broke the kiss.

"I say we pamper the lady in comfort," said Jack, the one holding her.

Trace nodded, a wicked light in his eyes.

Beth struggled to get loose, but Trace shook his head. He lifted the curtain to their bedroom to let Jack and Simon through. He quickly stripped off all his clothes. Jack passed her over as he followed Simon. Soon she was the only one dressed.

"I'll brush her hair," said Simon.

"I'll do her feet," said Jack.

Trace set her down on the bed. The noisy springs, ones she cursed every night after Trace filled her need with his own, creaked under her. He slid his hands under her skirt, raising the fabric to her thighs. Jack unbuttoned her boots and Trace unrolled her stockings. She stood facing her husband while Simon let her hair down and began brushing. She loved it when Trace brushed her hair, though he insisted she be naked first. He'd used the soft brush on other parts of her, too.

Trace suckled her through her gown as he flicked open her buttons. There were a few missing, thanks to his urgent need the previous night. She hadn't yet found them all to sew them back on.

"When Simon's finished with your hair, I'm going to cover your eyes," said Trace.

"Why?"

"So you won't know who's doing what."

She shivered. Would that be better or worse? If she didn't know who touched her, she couldn't feel as guilty. Not that she had anything to feel guilty about. Her husband wanted her to do this, and a man's word was law in his own home. Trace wanted her to enjoy being loved. With so few women in Montana Territory, perhaps other wives shared more than one man. It would be wonderful to have women friends.

Trace opened her gown and sent a trail of kisses down her front. Simon's strong arms brushed her hair from the top of her head to her bottom. She squeaked when Jack picked up her foot and suckled her toe. He winked and pressed a knuckle under the ball of her foot, causing her to sigh in relief. She hadn't realized how much her feet ached. Though she worked on her feet long hours at the farm, that was years ago. She hadn't been on her feet as much since. Jack's kneading removed knots she didn't know she had.

Jack stopped while Trace lifted her to stand, dropping her blouse and skirt on the floor. The evening breeze flowing in the window brushed past her hot flesh, cooling her. She was glad when Trace tied a handkerchief around her head and laid her on the bed on her back. That way she couldn't see them watching her with those hungry, possessive eyes.

She knew Jack held her foot and recognized Trace's wonderful kiss, so it must have been Simon who parted her lower curls with his tongue. He rubbed her clit. She pressed her feet down, pushing herself into his mouth for more. But he chuckled and began to tantalize her, flicking his tongue around and over, but never back on her clit.

Jack finished with her foot and worked his way up her leg to her thigh. The bed tilted as he moved around. At least, she thought it was Jack. Someone else kissed her. She tasted herself, so it must be Simon.

The bed squeaked in protest as they moved around and over her. She soon lost track of who was where. They discovered all her especially sensitive places—the outer curve of her breasts, under the back of her arm and the top of her thigh where her leg creased to her belly. They explored everything they could reach.

Then they turned her over and began again.

One man massaged her calves while another drew day-old bristles over her back, lightly scouring her and waking her skin. A third concentrated on her bottom, massaging her cheeks, pulling them apart, drawing fluid up from her pussy and pressing lightly.

How could anything that felt so good be wrong?

At an unknown signal, her hips were lifted and pillows inserted under her belly. Her face heated in embarrassment and desire as they positioned her with knees wide, bottom high in the air. Something cool spread between her cheeks before a finger slid just past her ring. Remembering how good it felt before, she pushed out.

"A ring of pink. Perfect," said a deep voice, either Jack or Simon.

She moaned when the finger pressed deeper, twisting to tantalize her. He slid in and out, adding another finger to stretch her again. Someone pushed the pillow aside and began playing with her pussy lips.

"Simon, on your back," croaked Trace.

The bed shifted beside her but the fingers kept up their work. She curved her back, thrusting her bottom high. A light spank caught her by surprise. She jerked, but a hand on her back kept her down.

"I'm going to lift you. Follow my lead," said Trace.

He helped her to kneel and then move over. Her leg touched a hairy thigh, tickling her. Trace lifted her again, settling her knees on either side of the rough thighs. She reached out to balance and found her hands pressing on a warm chest, her fingers catching curls.

When she leaned forward, a hard penis prodded her stomach.

"Don't bend it, darlin'. It could break," said the man under her. "Need help to find your ride? I remember how you like bareback."

Simon.

She grasped his cock, one fist over the other, making him moan. She lifted onto her knees, shuffled forward, and rubbed his cock against her, just where she needed. It wasn't enough. She leaned forward and placed one hand on his chest. Other hands guided her hips as she positioned Simon's long cock against her opening.

She slowly backed up, letting him slide in and out of her using short strokes. By the time he filled her, his gasps were louder than hers. She sat up, tall in the saddle. She jerked when rough fingers clasped her breasts from behind, catching her nipples between his fingers. Another set of hands grasped her hips, encouraging her to rise and fall.

She leaned forward, pressing her clit hard against his pubic bone. Finding the right angle, she drove him deep inside her, farther than ever before. She sped up, taking what she needed. Simon grasped her shoulders and pulled her down to his chest. She fought, wanting completion.

"Shh, Beth," whispered Trace. "Not yet. Trust me. It will be even better if you wait."

Someone settled behind her and spread something cool over her crack.

"Sweet and ripe, just like a peach," growled her husband.

He leaned forward, rubbing his chest hair over her back. For a moment she was sandwiched between their chests. He sat up and encouraged her to move forward. Simon's cock slid out part way.

"What are you doing?" she complained. "I was almost there."

"I'm going to do what I've wanted to since I first saw you, fists high, facing down Charlie in that jail cell."

He slid a finger deep in her ass. She clenched him, clenched them both.

"What's that?" she said, panting harder.

He leaned over her and skewered two more fingers in her.

"I'm going to fill your ass while you ride my brother," he growled.

He pressed his fingers in her bottom as he spoke. She felt wicked and wild with Simon already filling her. No one she'd ever met could know how wonderful this felt. She was raised to believe marital relations were something to be dreaded. But she'd found a husband who wanted her to feel pleasure. Even more, he wanted to increase her pleasure by sharing her with his brothers. She trembled, eager and scared at the same time.

"Will it hurt?"

"Sweetheart, we'll always take care of you. Did it hurt when I spanked you?"

"Yes!"

"But didn't it make you feel so good afterward?"

She bit her lip, not wanting to answer when she heard the laugh in his voice.

"Trust us, Beth. Trust us to know how to make you purr."

She hadn't yet made up her mind when he pulled out his fingers and pressed his cock against her. Simon twitched below her and she tightened up.

"Shh, relax. This is just like before, only more."

"That's easy for you to say," she bit out. "You're not the one being stuck!"

She bounced on Simon's chest when he laughed. His cock moved in her again, making her tingle.

"One of Lily's girls told me there's a walnut-size lump just inside a man," said Simon. "If you press it when he comes, it makes it even better. You should try it on Trace."

"Shut up, Sy," said Trace. "Don't be giving her ideas."

"Too late," she replied. "Your bottom goes up in the air next." Jack, off to one side, laughed, and she joined him, just a bit hysterical.

Trace grunted and pressed forward. She held her breath as he gently forced his way past her tight ring. For a moment it stung, and then she relaxed. Simon slowly rocked. She pressed on his chest to sit up. He let her rise just enough to grasp her breasts. She inhaled a gasp, and Trace pressed deeper. He pressed, in and out, a little farther each time.

"God, you're tight," he muttered when he completed her impalement. She tingled, panting as the two men set a rhythm. In and out, out and in.

Trace snuck a hand along her ribs and lifted her, holding her bottom tight to him. It allowed Simon to enter her pussy. While Trace filled her ass, Simon's cock rubbed forward and back against the thin membrane separating them.

She moaned as Simon plunged deep. He held her breasts tight in his fingers, squeezing until he exploded. He plunged upward, grunting. She soon joined him, quivering and gasping until he sagged back onto the bed.

Instead of letting her lie on top of Simon, Trace pulled her back tight against his chest. He entered her deeply, setting off more vibrations of pleasure. He lifted her. Simon moved out and away. Trace leaned back and shifted in the bed. When he stopped, she sat up, still connected. He pulled off her blindfold, and she blinked in the lamplight.

"My turn."

Jack's eyes flashed in the lamplight. His cock, slightly shorter than his brothers but thicker, like a sawed-off shotgun, throbbed for attention. She throbbed in return as he stepped close and rubbed the tip against her clit.

"This little lady's been ignored the past while," he murmured.

She looked down, watching his cock slip between her lips. He pressed himself against her, rubbing just where she needed, but tantalizingly slowly.

Trace throbbed in her behind. He set his hands under her cheeks and lifted her up and down, his massive strength controlling how her body moved.

When Trace lifted her almost off, Jack moved in. She pressed her shoulders back against Trace. She arched until her shoulders were the only part touching him above her bottom. Jack, facing her, slowly pumped with his hips. He used his fingers to pluck her nipples and caress her pussy lips.

His girth filled her even more than Simon. His fingers both soothed and vexed her, making her want more. Trace pulled her snug against him once more, and Jack sped up. His nostrils flared and eyes blinked rapidly as he stared at her. If she hadn't been so close to screaming in pleasure, he would have frightened her with his determined glare.

Trace took over her breasts, squeezing them, pinching her nipples. Jack rubbed her clit. She spasmed, unable to move but not needing to as each man took over.

Trace came first, bellowing into her ear as he exploded. She followed, then Jack slammed into her, bucking and gasping.

She was barely coherent when Simon helped Trace lift her off. She saw Jack leaning against the wall, panting hard, a jackal grin on his face.

Simon held her as Trace gently bathed her. He patted her dry and settled her under the sheets. She didn't move when Trace slid in behind her and pulled her close, spooning. She snuggled closer as he grasped her lower breast and sighed.

"My wife," he said, his voice grating on her ears, a sound she'd come to love.

Chapter Twelve

"Thanks for the pillow," said Beth to Jack the next morning. While Trace had set a folded blanket on the hard seat of the wagon, the pillow eased her tender bottom all the more. She smiled to herself. Tender, but worth it.

Acting the perfect wife, she sat beside Trace with her dress done up to her chin and her bonnet tied snug. Jack and Simon followed in the rented wagon, their horses tied behind. Less than one week from jail and she returned to town as a satisfied wife. She reveled in the crisp morning air, saying nothing. Simon and Jack nattered away.

When they passed the stream where she and Trace had celebrated, Simon whistled. She didn't turn around but he must have noticed her straightened back. He couldn't have seen her red face from behind.

"You'd better not be too sore to celebrate on the way home, Mrs. Elliott." Trace lifted an eyebrow in mock fierceness.

"Don't start with me, Mr. Elliott," she replied.

"Which Mr. Elliott you mad at, Beth?" called a voice from behind. "This is Jack speaking and, if it's Trace, I'd be mighty pleased to make you happy."

"I can make you even happier," called Simon. "I could make you so happy—"

"Keep that up if you want to sleep in the barn for the next few weeks," warned Trace.

"Yeah, yeah," said Jack. "You're just jealous 'cause she likes us best."

Beth's hot face flamed even more.

"I like you best," she whispered to Trace. She snuck her arm around his and leaned sideways for a moment.

"Hey!" yelled Jack in mock fierceness. "None of that flagrant displays of vulgar attention in town, you hear, Mrs. Elliott? We don't want to get thrown out again for fighting."

"We don't get thrown out for fighting, Jackass. We get thrown out for winning," said Simon. "Those miners think they're tough, but we always convince them otherwise."

The twins kept their voices down the rest of the way, allowing Beth to regain her equilibrium. But, when they approached the town, she began to tremble. She wrapped up the rifle in the blanket and placed the bundle on the pillow under the seat.

"Don't let those sniping biddies bother you," said Trace. "Keep your chin up and stare down at them." He turned and winked to her. "Should be easy as there's not too many taller. But don't leave the mercantile without one of us. I'll make sure Big Joe's not in town while you're inside with Patsy."

She straightened her spine and stared ahead. The bully would not scare her. Trace had complimented her on her dress, a new one she'd made. It had pretty blue and pink flowers on it, the pink matching her bonnet. She had clean stockings and boots on her feet and money in her reticule. And, for once, underclothes.

She waved as the twins headed to the livery stable. Trace stopped at Tanner's Mercantile. He held her waist and easily lifted her, setting her on the boardwalk. He lifted his hat to the few women on the street. Some blanched and hustled away, others nodded politely. Those ones looked at her with curiosity rather than scorn. Through the front window she could see a gaggle of women inside the store. She nodded politely to the old men enjoying the sunshine. The dog didn't lift his head, barely opening an eye as she passed.

Trace opened the door and ushered her inside. A few whispers, then silence. She ignored it, smiling up at her husband in thanks. She rested her hand on the arm he offered. They sashayed over to Patsy Tanner and the gossiping group of women they'd interrupted.

"Morning, ladies," said Trace.

Beth loved her husband's unmistakable growl but these women gaped at him as if he was part of a circus side show.

"Mrs. Elliott says there're a few things missing at the Rocking E," said Trace to Patsy. "Did you order that copper bathtub I asked for? My wife needs pampering, and it's first on the list."

He leaned over and kissed her, something not done in town. A quick peck wouldn't have been unusual in a just-married man, but he brushed his lips over her forehead before nibbling on her ear. He made it obvious that he'd much rather kiss her soundly, but had restrained himself.

He patted her bottom possessively before turning and sauntering to the back, whistling a cheerful tune. She stared, not having realized he could make such a lovely sound with his throat injury.

"That is one happily married man," said Patsy. She smiled and shook her head as she watched Trace.

"Well, I never!" huffed Mrs. Jennet. As usual, the banker's wife wore black bombazine and a scowl.

"You should try it sometime," said Beth, smiling as if he'd just pleasured her. "It makes all the hard work of caring for a husband worthwhile."

The other women stared at her as Mrs. Jennet clutched her bosom and gasped like a fish.

"I'll need six dozen canning bottles by the end of the month, Mrs. Tanner. Three men eat a lot. I don't know where they got the food in the pantry."

"Rowena Jones," said Patsy. "She and her late husband, God rest his soul, have the spread west from yours. She'll sorely miss the money she got from all the food those boys bought from her each fall. She's trying to get enough money to go back East to her daughter, but no one wants her place. Making preserves for single men is her only source of cash money."

"The garden I just started won't provide enough to get us through the winter. I expect Mr. Elliott will speak with her about provisions once again. My husband and his brothers are partial to her jams and pickles."

"I'm not surprised," said a pretty woman Beth hadn't seen before. Wearing peach silk, she was the best dressed. Delicate white lace dripped from her bodice and wrists. "Most men like a bit of sweetness and spice. Don't you agree, Mrs. Jennet?" The younger woman coughed into a scrunched handkerchief she held in her palm. "I hear you won blue ribbons for your spiced pears back East."

"I did, indeed. Perhaps someday you will aspire to such duties for your husband, Mrs. MacDougal. It must be difficult for him with you so unwell."

Her tone of voice and the way she sniffed made it obvious the banker's wife did not say it in concern but in condemnation.

"My husband is quite satisfied with the duties I perform," replied Mrs. MacDougal. She turned her back when a stronger cough hit her.

Mrs. Jennet pointed her eagle-beaked nose at the young woman's back. She glared as if Mrs. MacDougal had insulted her, but she wasn't sure about what.

"If it ain't Prudence MacDougal." A few ladies squeaked in surprise as Jack's honey-toned deep voice emerged from the back of the store. He looked Mrs. MacDougal up and down with his usual insolent grin. "The very woman who got the sheriff to keep us Elliotts from town."

A touch of color crept up the woman's cheeks. She dropped her eyes and brought her handkerchief to her lips.

"Jack Elliott, that is not how you speak to a young lady," said Mrs. Tanner. "Gillis's bride rarely gets to town. I won't have you ruin her day."

Jack swaggered over to the flustered group. He lifted his hat to the older women and winked at the younger. Before she knew what he was up to, he gave Prudence a peck on her cheek. Her pale cheeks flushed bright pink.

"Sorry, ma'am," said Jack. "I know it ain't your fault. But Gillis is no fun since he brought you home. I kinda miss those rip-roaring fights." He winked at Beth.

"No matter." Heads swiveled as Simon sauntered from the back room to stand beside Jack. He nodded politely to Prudence and tipped his hat to the ladies. "Since Trace got hitched, we can come to town whenever we like."

"I hear the sheriff might put the same rule on the other bachelor ranchers if they get rowdy," said Jack. He turned to Mrs. Jennet. "Get that banker husband of yours to toss a gold nugget into the pot. Maybe it'll encourage a few gals to ride the next Bride Train right to Tanner's Ford."

Simon swatted Jack on the back of the head. "Trace said to help load the wagon." He spoke to Beth while he selected a handful of penny candy sticks. "Got a letter from Ranger, the next brother down. He and Patrick are thinking of bringing a load of cattle north next year. Ben's almost finished his law training and he'll head home, too." He put a nickel on the counter and nodded to Patsy. "I remember that boy eating more than both of us together."

"Man's got a right to an appetite," replied Jack, winking at the women.

After lifting their hats to the women, both men left for the back lot, arguing about who got the peppermint stick. Beth fought to keep back embarrassment and laughter. The room stayed silent for a minute.

"Those Elliott boys have always been rude!" Mrs. Jennet sniffed, her head high. "Only a slattern would marry one of them!"

"Better an Elliott than Joe Sheldrake," said Patsy.

"My husband and his brothers are gentlemen," said Beth, ignoring the insult to herself. "They are kind and considerate, and take good care of me." She now knew Trace was not the poor man she thought she'd married. The Rocking E owed nothing to the bank. Therefore, she didn't have to bow down to the petty dictates of Mrs. Jennet and her cronies.

"If Trace Elliott is anything like my dear Gillis, you are a lucky woman," said Prudence to Beth.

"I am indeed." Beth turned to Patsy and held out her list. "Would you be able to fill my list, please? I believe these ladies have finished their business. Isn't that correct, Mrs. Jennet?"

Each woman sniffed at Beth as they swept out of the store after the banker's wife like flotsam caught in the wake of a pirate ship full of plunder. Prudence waited for the procession to pass. When the door closed with a snap, she turned to Beth. "I like your style with the old besom. Please, call me Prudence."

"And I'm Beth." They nodded pleasantly at each other.

"Unfortunately, I'm not able to come to travel much, but I would enjoy a visit," said Prudence. "My brother-in-law Nevin will be pleased that Ben is returning to Tanner's Ford. He's the same age as Ben and his twin, Ranger."

"Two sets of twins?" Beth gasped and pressed a hand to her belly. Having been married only a few hectic days, she hadn't thought about children.

"Perhaps you will be the same," said Prudence, mistaking Beth's shock for one of want. "My husband is also one of seven." She attempted a smile. "Gillis and I hope we will soon be blessed."

The door to the street opened and a huge man stood in the door. His head and face blazed as the sun lit his red hair and beard. In two strides he was at Prudence's side.

"There ye are, lovey. Time for a wee rest." She lifted her beaming face and received a chaste kiss on the cheek.

"You can do better than that, Gillis," she chastised him.

"I wouldn't want to embarrass you in front of the lady."

"Mrs. Elliott, I'd like you to meet my Scottish mountain of a husband, Gillis MacDougal. Gil, this is Beth, Trace's wife," said Prudence.

The huge man tilted his head and openly looked her up and down.

He was as bad as her husband and his brothers. It wasn't surprising if they'd been friends all their lives.

"Heard the auld man was forced to marry a hoyden Frank locked up. Choice of Trace or that blowhard Sheldrake." Bright blue eyes laughed into hers. "Trace must have two wives. I can't see this gorgeous creature putting her foot in a jail."

"Only one wife, thank you. It's true, I spent three horrid days in a cell," said Beth.

"If you're living with those Elliotts, ye won't mind seeing this."

Gillis gently brought Prudence close to him. She turned her flushed face up to him. He leaned down and proceeded to kiss her soundly. Beth, pleased someone else had a husband like hers, turned her back on the oblivious pair. She looked over the candy display until she heard the door close on the couple.

"Gillis looks at her as if she were candy," said Patsy, sighing after the two lovers. "Like Simon, he always had a sweet tooth."

"Thanks for the reminder," said Beth. "I'll need a few baskets of peaches when they're ripe." Patsy noted the request in her account book. "Mr. MacDougal seems to have a passion for life," said Beth quietly.

Patsy's lips quirked up. She looked over Beth's head toward the back room for a moment, then turned back. "I expect passion is something Elliotts have as well."

"Yep." A strong arm circled Beth's waist and pulled her back against a hard, tall body. A wave of heat rose from her lower belly at Trace's growled comment. Her nipples rose, unbidden, at his masculine smell of leather, horses, and ale. Trace rested his chin on her head and grasped her breasts.

Instead of being horrified, the older woman laughed. "You two newlyweds are worse than the MacDougals!" She fanned her face with her hand. "You'd better keep your hands off each other until you get out of town. You'll make everyone jealous. And if you see that husband of mine, tell him he'd better not tire himself out today!"

Chapter Thirteen

"Ben coming home?" Simon handed Trace a hundred-pound bag of flour.

Trace set it down with a thump, shaking the wagon. Beth, waiting on the seat, grabbed for a handhold. She didn't know much about the youngest four siblings but didn't want to ask questions as it seemed to bother Trace.

"He finished law school and is heading here instead of Texas. Don't know when but he'll bring things from Ma's estate."

"Tell him we don't want it," said Jack. "They threw Ma out without a penny."

Trace sighed. "I said the same thing until I got a wife."

She looked down, pretending to concentrate on smoothing her dress while listening intently to what Trace might say. How would she cope with yet another brother moving in?

"There might be pretty things Beth would like. You know, teacups and the like." Trace cleared his throat. "I won't deny our children because some rich old man hated to lose his daughter to Pa."

Simon grunted and stomped back into the store. She shifted slightly in her seat, glad she hadn't yet put on her bonnet. While still facing forward she watched Jack furiously pacing from the corner of her eye.

"If Ben wants to visit, he can eat and sleep in the barn. Otherwise, he can find himself a place in town. Since we broke down that wall upstairs there's no room for him," groused Jack. "I'm not giving up my bed, even if he is my brother."

"He's buying the widow Jones's property. We'll own the whole side of the valley." Trace lowered his voice to a loud whisper. "Three Elliotts is enough for Beth to handle. Ben's a lawyer now. He can take care of himself."

"You'll still be able to whup him, Jackass, while I do the same to Ranger," said Simon as he approached the wagon. "It'll be just like old times, the two of us against the two of them." He handed Trace the small, but heavy, cask of molasses he'd brought out. "I got something more important to know."

Trace placed the cask on the wagon and shoved it closer to the front. "What?"

"You think we'll have chicken and dumplings for Sunday dinner like Ma used to make?" Simon dropped his voice to a whisper. "Jack can clean up while I help Beth take a nap."

"If you're there, she won't sleep."

Beth turned around and glared at Jack, a finger held to her tightly closed lips.

"Shush! You two head home and get the chores done," ordered Trace.

Jack and Simon looked at each other, then Beth. Heat ran up her face. The two men glared at Trace.

"No stopping except to water the horses, hear?" Simon lifted a warning finger. Trace glanced at the clouds moving in.

"Nope. No time to dawdle today, boys."

He pulled out the oiled cloth. His brothers helped him roll it out and cover their goods. They went back in the store for a last load. Jack sauntered out with a pair of squawking chickens with their feet tied together. Beth understood why Simon asked about Sunday dinner.

Simon and Trace followed, each carrying a wriggling flop-eared dog.

"These are Old Walt's wedding presents," said Trace, frowning at the black and tan bundle in his arms. "Walt had Rosa keep them at Lily's until we came to town."

"Walt said they're Anthony and Cleopatra," added Simon with a straight face.

"Fool names for a couple of critters," growled Trace. Beth noticed he used both hands to carry the animal and didn't complain that it licked his chin. "This one's Tony." He made sure she had a secure grip before he released it.

"Tony and Cleo," said Beth, accepting the female from Simon. "I'll make Walt something sweet as a thank you." She held the puppies on her lap, but they were too excited to settle. While she was glad to have their company, there was a reason for the gift. A cat could catch mice and vermin, but dogs would bark to warn her when anyone approached. Old Walt was still watching out for her.

Trace climbed up beside her. One growl from him and the puppies huddled together, quiet. She sighed and shook her head, smiling to herself. They might be her dogs to care for, but they knew who was the leader of the pack.

Simon and Jack stayed near the wagon until they were well on their way home. Each man then took a sleeping dog on the saddle before him and set off toward the Rocking E. When they arrived in town, all three men strapped down their guns. She'd seen no one, not even Gillis MacDougal, doing the same. She waited to ask about it until the two of them were alone and Trace's vigilance had relaxed somewhat.

"Tell me what's going on."

"Nothing to worry about, Beth. You let us take care of you."

She slapped his shoulder. "If you won't treat me like an adult, Trace Elliott, I'm moving in with Rowena Jones. See if the three of you like being on your own again."

Trace's lip twitched at her growl but he kept silent.

"I have the right to know what concerns me." She watched him glower for a moment. "Big Joe's still mad at me, isn't he?"

"Nothing we can't handle." He winked, almost as insulting as a pat on the head. "We'll keep you safe."

She stared at him. "Oh, really?"

He nodded as if satisfied he'd said everything he needed to say to the little woman.

"What happens when all three of you are gone all day out in the fields or in the mountains chasing down cattle? There's little ol' me all alone at home, washing your socks, planting your garden, and preparing your supper. What if someone nasty comes calling? What then?"

"One of us is always nearby." His head settled lower on his shoulders.

"You can't get everything done with only two men."

"We'll figure something out," he muttered.

"Trace Elliott!" She slapped him hard on the biceps, then flapped her hand at the sting. "Why don't you trust me enough to tell me the truth?"

"You're a woman!"

She gasped loudly and looked at her lap. "Oh, my goodness, you're right. I've got breasts and there's nothing between my legs. How could I have not noticed?" She waited a moment until the path was smooth before scooting her pillow as far away as she could and still stay on the bench.

"A woman's not strong enough to take care of herself." Trace flicked the reins. The horses ignored him.

"I took care of myself in that jail. Look what I did with that ugly deputy when he tried to kiss me!"

"That was a lucky hit. If I didn't pull my gun on him, he would have smashed you to the floor with one blow."

She huffed but didn't deny the truth. "I'm strong enough to hold a rifle or shoot a pistol. A gun evens things out."

"Once you're out of shot, all he'd have to do was haul you on a horse and ride away."

Trace muttered to himself for the next few miles while Beth steamed. She used her time wisely, deciding how to decorate her new room—in the barn. She'd make the place comfortable with warm quilts. She'd get a thick door with a bolt on the inside. And she'd never serve anything sweet again.

"Aw, hell." Trace sighed and stared straight ahead. "Frank thinks Big Joe's joined the vigilantes. There's talk that the sheriff of Bannack City is the leader."

"The sheriff is leader of the road agents?"

Trace nodded. He twitched for a bit, keeping a close eye on the clouds slowly moving in, before settling. "One of Lily's girls heard Big Joe wants you used hard but still breathing." Trace looked down at her. A muscle jumped in his jaw. "After he lends you out to his friends for a while, he'll likely beat you to death."

Beth grabbed the edge of the seat to keep from swaying. She took a few breaths to settle her stomach. "He only wants to beat me? Why?"

"You don't want to know." He ground the words out between clenched teeth.

"Yes, I do!"

"Fine! He won't sully himself with you."

She crossed her arms under her chest. As usual, it caught his attention. She waited until he met her eye.

"Big Joe doesn't know words like 'sully.' What did he really say?"

"I will not use those words to my wife."

"Then use other ones. I want to know what he said."

Trace's jaw jutted forward for a moment. "He ain't gonna dirty his cock by putting it in an Elliott's, uh," mouth open, he flicked his eyes around, "in an Elliott." He gave a sharp nod. "Happy now?"

Beth couldn't get a breath. She used her hand to fan herself. Her stomach clenched into a hard ball. Beside her, Trace gripped the leather traces so hard his sun-browned hands turned white.

"Well," said Beth after a few minutes. "He doesn't want to rape me. At least we know the man does have limits."

"This isn't funny!"

"No, it isn't. But I'd rather laugh than cry." Suddenly chilled, she wrapped her arms around herself. "I don't know why you thought I'd be better off not knowing."

"I want to protect you, Beth," he said quietly after a moment. "You're my wife. It's my right and honor to keep you safe."

Beth looked up at his handsome face. The laugh lines were gone, deepened into stress cracks. She'd never had anyone protect her before, and she cherished his caring. But if someone wanted to do her harm, he'd wait until she was alone. For her own sanity, she wanted to protect herself, at least long enough for her men to come to the rescue.

"Thank you. But I also need to protect myself when you're not there. If I know how, I'll be less afraid." She glanced around. "There's bears, catamounts, and snakes out there. Poison and fever and accidents. I can't control any of that. Help me to learn to protect myself and our children. I may never need to pull that trigger. But if I do, at least I'd be prepared."

He inhaled, held his breath longer than she thought possible, and then gave an immense sigh. He muttered for a few minutes. She was sure she heard, "uppity woman," among the usual growls. Muttering was better than frigid silence.

"I was going to tell you about it," he said. "After we got home."

"You really think I'd believe that when I had to drag it out of you?"

"Dammit, woman! Why else would I buy you a rifle and pistol, and the ammunition to go with it? I sent out word I was looking for a dog to warn you if strangers approach the house. Walt took these off a miner before he could drown them."

"Walt deserves more than sweets for that. Perhaps I'll sew him a new shirt. You won't get jealous and shoot him if I give him a kiss on the cheek, will you?"

She tilted her head and looked up at him, fluttering her eyelashes.

Trace gave a snort almost as loud as a horse, not bothering to meet her glance.

"The man was ready to put his life on the line for you. He can have all the cheek kisses he likes for giving you a pair of guard dogs."

"How sweet! Guns and dogs, all for me."

He frowned down at her. "You funning me?"

"No, I'm happy for any presents, especially when they're useful. They'll help me take care of myself. When can I have my first shooting lesson?"

Trace looked down at her smiling face and shook his head. "You're as crazy as the rest of us." He snorted and the horses joined him. The one in front of Trace lifted its tail and released a load of dung. Trace's lip twitched. Beth coughed back a laugh.

"You in cahoots with that mare? Dang, let one female win and soon the whole barnyard's flapping."

Beth slid back close and nudged him, not too gently, with her elbow. He gave a loud *oof* as if she'd hurt him, then winked. He slapped the traces lightly and the horses increased their speed.

Beth sat still the rest of the way home, just enjoying having Trace next to her. She knew all three men cared about her. Because Bannack City was so wide open and wild, some people in Tanner's Ford felt they had to be extra strict as if to make up for the wickedness. Trace's easy affection would keep those biddies clucking for weeks. Patsy Tanner was right. The way Trace treated her made people jealous.

It wasn't only what Trace did to her body that made her want him. That was wonderful. She'd grown up without anyone caring about her. Maybe that was why she wanted it so badly. Having three strong men protecting her was nice. The way they pleasured her was wonderful.

But it wasn't love.

She'd known the quiet, demanding, arrogant man beside her for less than a week. Yet she knew him better than she had anyone in her life, maybe even herself. She loved him, body and soul, but he couldn't love her back. Wouldn't. She was falling for Jack's boyish eagerness and Simon's calm depths as well. Would they love her, if Trace couldn't?

No matter. She'd make do. What she had now was far more than she could ever have dreamed of. The fact that she wanted more, was her little secret.

Chapter Fourteen

"Simon and Jack will be right unhappy when they come home to only one pie between them," said Trace. "They saw the bucket of berries you picked and they'll think pies for dinner, supper, and breakfast."

"They have no reason to complain. There's also a pot of stew and lots of leftover biscuits to go with it."

Beth turned around once more to make sure her four precious pies were safe. She'd set them on an old Hudson's Bay blanket in a shallow box. It would stop them sliding on the wooden floor of the wagon and help keep them warm.

"Those two always bicker. Ranger and Ben are also twins but I don't remember them going at each other like that."

"You said Prudence MacDougal isn't well enough to pick berries or make pastry. She was kind enough to invite me for a cup of tea. I will not be shamed by arriving without something special in return."

"Guess I gotta get down on my knees and thank God again for sending me to town that night. It would break my heart to think some other lucky man had you in his bed every night and your cooking in his stomach every day."

Beth twisted her mouth sideways and raised her eyebrow at her husband. "I think there was a compliment somewhere in there. Don't get all sentimental on me, now."

Unable to touch her while using both hands to guide the horses, he nudged her with his elbow. "A man better say something nice to his wife when he's taking her to visit a couple of bachelors."

"I'm visiting Prudence, not anyone else."

Trace turned to her, one eyebrow raised. A smile played around his lips. "Sweetheart, as soon as those boys see my pretty wife and smell those pies, you'll be overrun by Scots."

"Are they all large and red like Gillis?"

Trace shook his head. "Gillis had a different mother. Phoebe died at Fort Laramie birthing Louisa." He sighed. "Finan MacDougal took his screaming daughter and rode out to the Indian camp to find a woman."

"His wife was barely in the ground and he wanted another one?"

"He had a hungry baby girl with no ma or milk for her. He didn't want to lose both wife and babe."

"What happened?"

"Sunbird's man was killed when she was only a few months along then her baby boy was born dead. After that, no man wanted her as a wife. When she heard Fin's baby crying she rushed over, in pain from too much milk. After she fed the babe and both felt better, Fin set her on his horse and led them back to the fort. No one read the Book over them, but they're still together."

"What did your mother think of all this?"

"She had to accept it as Jessamine decided to be born. Sunbird knows healing. She delivered Jess that night, Ranger and Ben the following year, and Patrick two years after that."

Beth let the information sink in as Trace wrestled the wagon across the creek. She hadn't had her monthlies since arriving in town. As far as she knew, it was the only way to tell if a baby was growing inside her. Perhaps next time she went to town she could ask someone about it, but who? If she was blessed with a child, who would help her with the birth?

Neither spoke as the wagon rose up the far side of the creek. The MacDougals held the M-D Connected right across the valley from the Rocking E. It was one reason Rowena Jones was happy to sell her ranch to Ben rather than a stranger. No one could pass through the valley without both families knowing.

"Elliott, ye auld coot! Ye finally smartened up and found a wife."

Birds erupted from the trees behind the log home at Gillis's booming welcome. He wiped his forehead. He wore a homespun shirt, socks, and boots. Between his waist and hairy knees was a kilt of thin blue and green bands over red. A wider band, showing large squares of red with thin white lines, circled his hips.

With an ease Beth found unsettling, he stuck the huge ax into the chunk of tree he used as a chopping block. His reddish-orange hair flamed just as bright as she remembered. The hem of the kilt swung side to side as he strode over.

"Was waiting for the right one." Trace slowed the horses to a stop. "The twins won't like Beth giving away her baking to the lot of you."

"Baking?" Gillis sniffed. His bright blue eyes crinkled, and a wide smile showed white teeth between his bushy moustache and beard. "Berry pies?"

Beth climbed off the seat and knelt in the back of the wagon. She touched the edge of a pie. Still warm, but not so hot she couldn't pick it up.

"Trace said you lived with your wife and two brothers. We brought one pie each." One by one, she placed all four on the wagon seat.

"Come visit any time you like," said Gillis, licking his lips. He winked and lifted a pie in each large hand. "Lift your wife down so she can visit Pru, and we can have at these pies."

"Not until dinner!" Beth shook her finger at both men. They pouted, grinned at each other like five year olds, and then nodded. Trace lifted her down and followed her into the house, carrying the last set of pies.

"Elliotts and MacDougals help each other all the time," said Trace. "That's why our homes are the same, Pa and Fin built them together."

"Not quite the same," whispered Beth. "*They* have a wooden door on their bedroom rather than a curtain!"

"Ah, but Nevin and Malcolm are a wee bit shy," said Gillis, not bothering to pretend he hadn't heard. He set his burden on the kitchen table. "They're not like Simon and Jack." He winked, then laughed when heat rose up her face. "About time those lads found some good luck." He waited for Trace's hands to be free before slapping him on the back, hard. "How ye been, old man?"

"You don't want me to upset Pru by showing her how I can still grind your face into the mud."

"She's been moody the last few days. Mayhaps it would make her laugh. But warn me first. I wouldnae want to dirty me kilt."

"If I've been moody, you've been a fair grump, Gillis MacDougal." With a swish of soft fabric, Prudence entered the room. "Out of my kitchen," she said. She made shooing motions to the two giant men.

"We've got our marching orders," said Gillis. He shook his finger at his wife. "Don't eat all the pie, my love. I'm already hungry." He gently kissed her cheek and pushed Trace out the door.

"He's always hungry," said Prudence. She smiled at Beth. "Shall we have tea, or would you prefer black current cordial?"

"Cordial would be lovely."

As Prudence filled two slender glasses, Beth spent a few minutes entranced by the picture quilts hanging from the parlor walls. She admired the rich ruby color of the cordial before sipping. The sweet berry tang erupted in her mouth. It was so good she drank more.

"I've never seen such beautiful art," said Beth. "You must spend hours sewing."

"I'm not physically strong, but I can work with my hands. I also tat lace." She held up one hand to show the froth of white edging her cuff.

"It's beautiful and finer than anything I've seen back East."

Prudence beamed. "Would you like some? I have plenty to choose from."

"Oh, I couldn't."

"Elizabeth Elliott, you brought my hulking husband four hot pies. That's worth a few inches of lace!"

"Thank you," said Beth. "I could use some to edge a special nightgown I'm sewing."

"You wear nightgowns in bed?"

Beth remembered the deep kiss she saw Pru share with her husband in Patsy's store. Beth needed another woman who could understand her life. Who else but the wife of her husband's dearest friend?

"Not for long," she whispered. She held her breath.

Pru's face colored deep pink. "Gill is so eager some evenings I finally made one with a tie at the throat. One pull and I'm all his," she whispered back.

Their eyes met, sharing understanding. One started snickering, then the other. They toasted each other and sipped. Pru offered Beth a seat on an upholstered sofa someone had hauled a long way west. They soon set their empty glasses on the table in front of them.

"This is lovely cordial," said Beth. "I feel rather lightheaded."

"Isn't it grand? I fear Mrs. Jones adds quite a dose of spirits, but it is a treat." She filled both their small glasses. They sipped contentedly for a few minutes.

"I will have to get her recipe." Beth smiled at Prudence. "Thank you for inviting me. You've got more color today than when we met in the mercantile. Are you feeling better?"

"The heat and dry air are good for my lungs. I have more energy too," she said, blushing, "to do what one does to become a mother."

Beth returned Prudence's hopeful smile, pleased the other woman was just as honest and open. "That should make your husband very happy."

"Yes and no. His mother died in childbirth. He thinks I might as well."

"What do you think?"

Pru looked out the window, blinking hard. "I think I can have a baby. But I'm not strong enough for the West. I thought I was, but I was a fool. And now it's too late. I'm married to a wonderful man whose life is in Montana Territory."

"Wouldn't he move East to care for you?"

"He would do anything for me. Anything." Pru raised both her eyebrows. "Can you see Gillis in a stuffy Boston parlor? That big, hairy, orange man with his booming voice and Scottish accent?" She shook her head. "Gillis needs to live here, where he grew up. I've had this cough so long I know it will never leave. Even if we moved East, I'd only live a few years longer." She turned away, quickly blinking.

Beth said a silent prayer while her new friend settled herself. "If there's any way I can help, anything at all, I'll do it for you."

"Thank you." Prudence took a deep breath. "I have a younger sister, Amelia. She's four years younger than I and much smarter." Prudence shrugged. "My sister doesn't do silly things like run away to find adventure, marry the first handsome man who asks for her hand, and follow him into the wilderness."

"Is she married?"

Pru shook her head. "Amelia's face was burned when she rushed in to rescue a child from a neighbor's burning home. It took a long time to heal. She thinks she's hideous to look at, that no man would ever want her. She has some scarring on one side of her face but so do many others." Pru smoothed her skirt. "I know she wants children, but she won't look for a husband."

"If she takes the Bride Train, she's bound to find one."

Pru shook her head. "She refuses to show her face to strangers. In any case, she says she won't leave one home before knowing she has another."

"I can understand that. My stomach was in knots every minute until Trace first put his arms around me. Only then did I feel safe."

"You're much taller than Amelia. She'd be even more frightened. I suggested she marry Gillis's younger brother, Nevin. She's eighteen, he's nineteen, and neither one of them are likely to marry otherwise.

He won't go East and she won't come West without a husband. Gillis said they could marry by proxy. I suggested Amelia bring a companion with her on the train, an older woman, one who knows more about the dangers a young, shy woman would face. Perhaps a widow who wishes to come West for a better life."

Beth thought of all the nights she curled in the corner of the rail car. At first it was fun to chat with the other women but as brides left the train, the car filled up with others. Some of the men thought the women were eager for men. Beth always kept a few hat pins within easy grasp. With a companion, they could sleep in shifts, one protecting the other.

"Having a friend would have made my journey far more pleasant," said Beth. "Is Nevin like Gillis?"

A ladylike snort emerged from Prudence. "Pardon me, but when you meet Nevin, you'll see why I laugh. All they have in common is their father's bright blue eyes. Gillis is big, red, loud, and hairy. Nevin has a lot of his mother in him. Dark hair, and little of it, unlike my bear of a husband. Nev is quiet but solid."

"If your sister is shy, she may prefer that type of husband."

"Amelia's only shy with strangers, but yes, Nevin would suit her." Pru played with the lace on her sleeve. "If someone tried to hurt me, Gillis would rage and roar, killing them with whatever was close at hand. Nevin would first make sure I was safe. He'd fade into the forest and go after them, knowing Ross would stay and keep us safe. Only when he'd found them, faced them with what they'd done, and helped them leave this world, would he return."

"I can see Trace reacting like Gillis, and Simon like Nevin. And Jack?" Beth looked at the floor for a moment. "Jack's a charmer. Once he made sure I was safe, he'd go after them. He'd find a way to get close without them discovering who he was. I can see him setting them up, maybe forcing them into a draw, and killing them openly. No one would know why except the two of them."

Both women sat for a moment, thinking as they sipped.

"I do apologize. This is not a subject for afternoon tea, is it?" said Prudence.

"We aren't silly misses in a stuffy parlor back East. We're surrounded by miles of treacherous mountains and worse miners, the only brides within fifty miles. Whatever we say stays between us."

"I do like you, Elizabeth Elliott." Prudence lifted the half-empty bottle from the table. "More cordial? After all, we are celebrating your wedding."

"Yes, please!"

After filling their glasses Prudence tilted her head and looked at Beth.

"I want Amelia to find a husband who cares for her no matter what. I think she and Nevin are right for each other."

"What do they say?"

"Nevin is agreeable. In fact, he's rather eager to meet her." She hesitated a moment. "You see, because of Amelia's face, she doesn't judge people by their looks. Nevin and Ross are sensitive to that. But, while Ross rebels, flaunting his differences, Nevin withdraws."

"They are dark like their mother, Sunbird."

"Yes." Pru twisted her damp handkerchief around her fingers. Her eyes moved around the room, not settling.

"There's something else, isn't there? Please, you can ask me anything," said Beth.

A flush rose from Pru's snug collar. "Do you mind if I undo this top button? The men won't return until I ring the dinner bell."

Beth nodded and flicked open her own tight collar. Since marrying Trace, she rarely wore anything constricting. She'd even debated whether to wear drawers under her petticoats but decided on decorum. Trace had snorted but not refused her. Good thing, as she was learning to do as she chose no matter what he said.

"That's better," said Pru, waving her hand in front of her face. Like Beth, she'd opened more than one button. "Gillis says you're a good wife to the Elliott men." She caught Beth's eyes. "Not just

Trace, but his brothers."

Beth knew this would happen but not when. A flash of heat hit her from both embarrassment and arousal from recent memories. She was now the one smoothing her skirts with trembling hands.

"You knew this, yet you invited me into your home?"

"MacDougals and Elliotts have stood beside each other since they met in 1844. My in-laws raised four Elliotts in Texas. The ones I've met are decent men. I will not deny myself the friendship of another woman who does not care if she ruffles the feathers of those biddies in town. We are friends?"

"Friends." Beth exhaled the breath she hadn't realized she'd held. "And thank you. From our one meeting, I thought you wouldn't be too judgmental, but one never knows."

"Given the choices you had to make, I believe you chose well. You certainly look happy with Trace."

"I am, when I'm not trying to knock his head off his stubborn, manly shoulders."

The two young women shared a relieved laugh.

"When I die, will you help Amelia?"

"Oh, Pru, don't say that."

"I want to have a baby." She rested her hand on her flat belly. "Some nights I lie awake worrying I might not be able to raise my child because of my cough."

"Accidents and sickness can happen anytime, to anyone." Beth gently touched Prudence's knee. "You must have heard that Trace's parents died of a spring fever when he was sixteen and the youngest only ten. We have no control over what God sends us. Since you know you are ill, you will take better care of yourself."

Prudence's expression lightened. "Thank you for that. But if Amelia marries Nevin, my baby will have a mother and maybe an aunt as well. My only concern is that my husband will be without a wife." She raised her chin and looked Beth in the eyes. "If I sicken, before I die, I want Amelia to promise she'll try to share herself with

Gillis and Ross. Once she meets them, I know she'll care for them as much as I do. But she needs to know that someone else, someone wonderful like you, does the same."

The cordial reduced Beth's reaction to Pru's statement. She heard the words yet did not feel shocked.

"Do you share yourself with your brothers-in-law?"

Pru shook her head. "I told Gillis I would if he wished, but Nevin said no." A flush rose on her cheeks. "I love my husband very much. But I also love his brothers. They are so different yet they all attract me. Nevin and Ross have lovely, smooth copper skin. Sometimes I watch them. The way their muscles move when they work hard. How their long fingers run along the flanks of their horses."

"They make you feel a bit like Gillis does."

"Yes. But Nevin won't touch a white man's wife." Pru folded her hands carefully on her lap. "Gillis says Nev would do whatever his wife wished. They've spoken of it, all three of them. They are close, and already share so much. If Gillis was alone and Amelia was willing, the three brothers would care for her as your men do you."

Prudence clasped Beth's rough hands in her thin ones. "If something happens to me, please speak to Amelia. If she is not horrified, please tell her how right this is for you. I believe a family is whatever one chooses it to be. Out here we must make our own rules. Caring for more than one man to make a family strong cannot be wrong."

Beth nodded. "I agree. The people who raised me never cared whether I lived or died unless I was of use to them. Since I married Trace, I've discovered such..." She blinked and turned her face away.

"You love him, don't you?"

"Yes. Body and soul. I also love Simon and that rascal Jack. I know they care for me. Trace may even love me a little, but he'd never admit it." She took a moment to steady herself. "Trace was terribly hurt when his parents died and left him to cope with six younger siblings. He refuses to feel that way again. I believe Simon and Jack love me, but until Trace declares his love, they keep their feelings to themselves."

"Aren't we a pair? You're in love with a man who's sworn not to return it so he won't be hurt. I'm already hurting Gillis because he knows he'll lose me when I die. Yet neither of us would change our lives." She picked up her glass. "Other than wishing that my lungs worked better," she murmured.

"Consumption?"

"No. I've always had a weak chest. I was silly and got wet one night when I snuck out of the house as a girl. I developed a cough but never took care of it. I didn't want my parents to know I'd misbehaved again. Since then, every winter I get worse."

"I'm so sorry."

"Don't be. I had the adventures I wanted. It's Gillis who will need you. Will you do what I ask? Encourage Amelia to live her life as you do?"

"Considering the wonderful life I've found, how could I do anything else?"

Chapter Fifteen

"Where are you taking me?"

"We're going for a ride," replied Trace. "You haven't been out of the house since we visited the MacDougals."

Beth swatted the hand caressing her bottom, but it didn't stop moving. She hadn't worn trousers before, but they were better for riding than her skirts. The way the center seam rubbed against her made her feel wicked. Her husband's roving hand heated her further.

"It's a surprise." Trace swept her into his arms. Though she kicked her feet and pounded on the arms holding her, all he did was laugh. He turned her sideways to pass through the door and into the morning sun.

"Mornin', darlin'," drawled Jack. He held the reins of Peaches, the old bay mare Trace had bought from Rowena Jones for her to ride.

Beth narrowed her eyes. She'd been married almost two months. She'd learned enough about her men to know such an innocent look meant trouble was brewing.

"What is this all about?"

"You'll like it, Beth," said Simon. He held the reins to Trace's gelding. He nodded to her unspoken question.

"Fine! Don't tell me."

She'd learned to trust Simon's word most of all. Trace still tried to protect her by withholding information, telling her she didn't need to know the answer. Jack hid his seriousness behind charm and flattery. Neither lied, but only Simon, a solemn, deep thinker, said what she needed to know. Trace set her onto her saddle. She leaned forward and patted the patient mare. "We females will stick together, won't we, Peaches?"

Trace climbed on Sailor, his massive brown and white gelding. The paint was distinctive, both an advantage and disadvantage. When one of his brothers rode the horse, no one knew if it was Trace with his lightning-fast trigger finger, or one of his only slightly slower brothers.

"Those chores better be done before I get home or there'll be hell to pay."

"Don't teach a hound to suck eggs," said Jack. He turned his back on them and stomped into the house.

"Simon, please tell me Jack's not cooking tonight. With this heat, I'm not up to greasy stew and burned biscuits."

"Trust us, Beth." Simon handed her the reins and made sure her feet were set right. "Make sure the big guy doesn't tire you out too much." He turned to Trace. "And keep her out of the sun."

"Enough!" Trace nudged Sailor. Peaches, always eager, followed.

Beth concentrated on her lessons for the first few minutes. Heels down, shoulders back, head high. She'd attached a scarf to her riding bonnet that protected her shoulders and neck from the mid-summer sun. She knew she looked ridiculous wearing a man's shirt and pants along with a pink bonnet, but it got the job done, as Trace would say.

The previous times they'd gone riding, they'd gone downhill toward the river. This time Trace headed up. Peaches, as if sensing adventure, danced sideways before Beth proudly settled her again. Warm and sunny, it was a glorious day to escape her chores.

If only she could convince Trace to do something about their bedroom. Though they hid it, she saw the yearning in both Simon and Jack's eyes when Trace swooped her up and carried her off to sleep. Sometimes they'd cuddle, quietly talking, for twenty minutes.

Trace was her legal husband, but Simon and Jack needed her affection as well. As twins, they'd always had each other, but now and then one would hug her for a few moments when no one else was near. Nothing to heat her blood, but it warmed her heart. Trace clung to her some nights, just for her touch. Simon and Jack must have needed someone to hug as well. But the twins wouldn't intrude between them.

Because Trace was so large, there was barely room for the two of them in her bed. If Simon or Jack tried to sleep there as well, she'd either get squashed or end up sleeping on top of one of them. Considering how they snored when flat on their backs, placing her head on a loud chest would not help her sleep.

They rose steadily, Trace pointing out ways to mark their path. Now and then a golden eagle soared above them. Trace finally stopped by a rock face and frowned. She caught up to him. He pointed to one part, then the other. It looked liked the rock had been cleft by jagged lightning, and one half pushed back.

"Yep. This is it." He got down from Sailor and reached up to take her. He held her for a few minutes until her legs steadied. "You're doing well. This is the longest you've ridden yet."

Beth looked around the small clearing but saw nothing special. The brook they'd been following ran along one side. She walked over to it and sat on a flat rock. She splashed cool water on her face. When she turned back, Trace was gone.

Her heart pounded and she forced it to slow. No, not gone. He wouldn't have left her alone up here. Sailor quietly cropped grass beside Peaches, proving nothing was amiss. A moment later, dark green bushes shook and Trace stepped out from what she'd have sworn was solid rock. He held out his hand to her.

After hobbling the horses, he guided her through what was indeed a narrow cleft. They passed between the rocks and stepped into a closed meadow. Only then did she hear the roar of the waterfall.

"It's beautiful!"

The brook arched over a round rock about twenty feet high. The sun made rainbows in the mist. Most of the water landed on broken rocks before rushing downhill and away. Lush growth lined the meadow walls. Underneath a dappled canopy far enough from the waterfall to stay dry, lay a bedroll. Beside it was a lumpy flour bag.

Was that the bag she'd looked for yesterday? She frowned at Trace. He strolled over to the bedroll and held his arms out to her, a determined smile on his face. Her breasts responded, swelling to fill his hands. They'd been too busy lately to play. Each night they fell into bed exhausted, then crawled out before sunup early the next morning.

She swore she'd bottled more green and yellow beans than the entire town could eat in a year. Rowena Jones, delighted to help the young Elliott bride in exchange for cash money toward her trip back East, had shaken her head at the amount the men needed. Trace must have realized how eager she was to escape the hot kitchen.

"Adam and Eve, in the Garden of Eden," he said. "Race you."

He pulled his loose shirt off over his head and tossed it aside. Giving up on buttons, Beth threw off her bonnet and did the same. She dropped to the grass and unlaced her boots. Socks were tossed aside immediately after. They froze, right hands on their belts and smiled into each other's eyes.

Without changing where they looked, they unbuttoned and dropped their pants. Beth's dropped easily once she pushed them over her hips. Trace's got hung up on the arrow pointing at her.

"I need help, wife," he growled.

She dragged her toes and swayed her hips with each slow step toward him. His nostrils flared as she approached. His eyes devoured her body. She stopped a few feet away and shook out her hair. He licked his lips. She slid her palms up from her waist, over her breasts, and behind her neck. She caught up her hair and lifted the mass. Her breasts rose as well, jutting out proud and free.

He growled and kicked his pants aside. She stood there, one knee bent to coyly cover herself. He stalked forward. One step. Two. Then he reached around her and captured her bottom in his hands. He pulled her tight so his cock pressed against her belly.

"Mine," he growled.

She sighed into his kiss. She released her hair, wrapping her arms around his neck instead. The hair on his chest rasped against her breasts with the merest touch of pain. She nipped his nipple and then licked it. He moaned in response.

Nibbling his skin the whole way, she slowly dropped to her knees. She wrapped her hands around him, leaving the thick purple head free. He rocked his hips forward and back to encourage her.

"Mmm. Haven't seen this fellow up close in a long time." She tilted her head and looked up at him. "I'm hungry." She licked his tip and was rewarded with a drop of salty fluid. His deep groan was all the encouragement she needed. She sucked him deep in her mouth, then pulled back, letting her teeth gently glide along his length.

"Oh, God, Beth! I can't stop."

She pulled away long enough to whisper, "Then don't," before engulfing him again. He grasped her head and pressed her close, thrusting against her. She controlled his depth with her fists, shafting him even as she sucked. His deep groan warned her. She swallowed him as deep as she could. He bucked against her, gasping. She held tight until he slowed, savoring the taste of him.

"Whoa, where did *that* come from? I've got to sit down but I can't move!" He trembled, gasping and laughing at the same time. She released him and backed away, smiling and licking her lips. He fell to his knees on the bed, then his back. "C'mere, wench."

She curled up against him, her head resting on his right shoulder. He held her tight as his violently racing heart slowed to mere excitement.

"After that, I need a nap." He looked around. "We're in the shade. Wake me when you're hungry again." He settled his arms around her and dropped off. Just as tired, she got comfortable and joined him.

* * * *

Trace watched the witch softly snoring on her back beside him.

She had to be a witch. Why else would he spout poetry and explode into her eager mouth like a fourteen year old? He shook his head. He'd damn near passed out when he came that time. He picked a flower from the grass and drew it across her nipple. It immediately crinkled. He smiled and touched the other. It responded the same.

"Mine," he whispered.

His brothers understood why he had to get her away. Just the two of them. Things would be different when they returned home, and he wanted these memories fresh in his woman's mind.

His woman, to keep and to share.

He rested his palm above the golden curls that hid her sweet perfume. Was his child growing in her yet? No matter who planted the seed, the first babe would be his. She twitched in her sleep. He kept still until her breathing deepened once more.

What was it about this cantankerous female that made him want to hold her close so she'd never be hurt? He'd once spent most of a week with a comely whore in Virginia City. An hour after he left, he couldn't have said what she looked like other than blonde with big tits and teeth.

One look at his Beth in the dim glow of a sheriff's lantern and she was branded on his mind.

Her image and laugh kept him going during the long summer days. He had thought a clean house and good food would be enough. But Beth's welcoming smile eased all his aches and pains. Sometimes he heard her singing when she thought no one was near. His voice was wrecked but his ears worked fine. He thought they were hymns but the woman couldn't carry a tune in a basket. He'd never tell her that. Days when she sang, their loving was eager and explosive.

He wet his finger and touched it to her nipple. When he blew, it tightened into a tight nubbin. When she woke, he would tease her with his moustache. He'd drag it over her belly and thighs, nibbling every morsel of her. He'd lick her juicy folds until she'd scream in aroused frustration.

His cock swelled, eager to do his bidding.

"Why don't you put your mouth where it will do the most good?"

He looked down and smiled. "You're awake."

"Awake and hungry. What's in the flour bag you took from my kitchen?"

"Bread and cheese." He trailed his moustache over her breasts. She pressed up into him. "You want food, or me?"

"I can get food at home."

"I hoped you'd say that. Show me where to start."

First she stretched, arms and pointed toes straight. She rolled onto her stomach, then knees. "Give me a minute in the bushes first."

He admired the way her bottom jiggled with every step. She'd put on a few pounds since she arrived and was far better for it. She came out of the bushes, one hand splayed across her belly. Shoulders back, she sashayed over to him like the finest madam in Virginia City.

"Whadda you want, cowboy?" She lifted her breasts to him. "These?" She turned around, spread her legs, and bent over. Her sweet swollen lips parted for him "Or this?"

He knelt, clasped his cock and slowly rubbed up and down, enjoying her wild playfulness. "What else you got?"

She walked until they were mere inches apart. He inhaled her scent, rising from just under his nose.

"You can have whatever you find."

"I want two of those," he pointed to her breasts, "two of these," he reached around and clasped a buttock in each hand, "and this." He bent slightly and rubbed his smooth chin against her mound.

"Mmm, I think we can come to a deal. Do you pay in gold like the miners?"

"Play now, talk later, pay last."

He slipped his hands down her legs and pulled. She collapsed but he caught her and laid her back on their bed. Blonde hair tumbled around her head and over her front. "God, Beth. What you do to me."

He suckled one nipple, then the other as she groaned in

agreement. He slid a finger into her and curled it forward.

"I want you now," she growled, eyes flashing up at him. "Deep inside me. Hard!"

He shook his head. "I'm going to stoke you so high you won't know where you are. You'll beg me to take you hard. And you'll scream my name when you come."

He covered her mouth with his before she could reply.

Chapter Sixteen

"I swear, Trace Elliott, you will eat nothing but lumpy porridge and burned biscuits in the morning for the next thirty years." His tongue flicked on her bud. "Oh, yes. There!"

He immediately slid away from the spot.

"Oh, you terrible man." Beth panted for a moment, gathering her strength. Flat on her back in the hidden meadow, she looked down her body at him. Dark eyes grinned over her mound, her curls providing a blonde moustache.

"I won't let you touch me again before the snow flies."

Trace inserted a finger and rubbed it against a wonderful place. She curled her fists and toes to stop herself from thrusting up to demand more. She clenched her teeth, but a low moan still escaped. He flicked her clit with his tongue and hummed.

The wonderful spiral of white-hot need spun tighter. She writhed, unable to control the moans and growls that escaped her. There! She was—

He sat up, leaving one broad hand flat on her belly. His face from nose to chin glistened in the sun. He panted as hard as she. But he grinned in triumph while she howled in frustration.

"Beg me," he growled. "Beg me to take you hard!"

"No!" His cock, hard and red, showed he was as close as she. "No, I won't. You want this too."

He curled his hand around his thick cock. "I can take care of myself. You can't."

"I can, and will, as soon as I get home. Simon and Jack will do everything I want. Twice!" She struggled to get up, but his palm kept her pinned.

"Not if I tell them to stay away."

His calm words cut though the need pulsing through her veins. She stopped struggling and looked at him. No emotion showed on his face. It was as if they were in town and the mayor or banker was near. His cock drooped, a measure of emotion he couldn't hide. Would he do that to Simon and Jack? He was the one who encouraged them to touch her.

Her husband had brought her here for a reason. She caught a flash of yearning before he turned his face away. It wasn't the waterfall that entranced him. He wanted something from her. Something more than her body.

She told him when they married she did not want to be just a body to be used. Did he think that was all he was to her? A method of protection and joy easily replaced by two brothers? If so, he was wrong.

"Does anyone else know of this place?"

He hesitated and then shook his head.

"Thank you for bringing me. It's beautiful."

He shrugged. "So are you." He lifted his hand from her belly but she didn't move.

"Trace, look at me. Please."

When he met her eyes, his were hooded.

"Trace Elliott, I have something to tell you."

He stiffened.

"You are my husband, in law and the church." He stared as she spoke, his chest barely moving. "And also in my heart."

Nothing moved but his eyelids. She'd learned he blinked hard when hiding strong emotions.

"I love you. I know you said you can never do the same. Knowing you wanted me to see something so precious to you is enough for me." She sighed heavily. "Even when you make me scream in frustration, I still love you."

His cock grew, stretching toward her. "Aw, sweetheart," He croaked. He brushed strands of her hair out of her eyes, tucking them behind her ear. With the back of his knuckles he brushed her nipples, which she hadn't realized had also softened. "You're not just saying that because I won't let you come unless you beg me?"

The laugh lines were back, outlining his dark eyes. She rolled her head from side to side in an exaggerated "no". His sigh seemed to come from so far down in his chest that it rattled his ribs when leaving. He closed his eyes and pressed his forehead against hers.

"Sweetheart, I can't..."

"Shh, it's all right," she said. She ran her fingers through his hair as one day she might their child. Lovingly and with no demands.

"Do you love the twins, too?" She felt the tension in the lost-little-boy question.

"Yes, but not the same as you. You're my husband. The first man who let me be who I am. You'll always be first in my heart. But Simon and Jack need me, too. I see their hurt when you take me to bed, excluding them. They want what we have. But until you prove to them that you're not jealous, they won't ask for more."

"Can you love three men the same?"

"No, not the same," she replied, "but equally."

He frowned but didn't reply.

"You are all different people and I love different things about you. Simon's deep and quiet. One wink from him means more than ten minutes of Jack's loving blather. But get Jack alone and he's quiet and earnest."

Trace picked a grass stem and chewed for a moment. "Have they touched you without me there?"

She shook her head. "Other than a light hug during the day, no. They love you so much, they'd go without rather than chance hurting you."

"I'm not jealous of Simon and Jack loving you."

"I don't know how you can prove it when we sleep alone in our bedroom each night."

"You don't mind bedding Jack or Simon without me?"

"No, but you have to first prove to all of us that it is what you want."

He looked at her for a moment before his eyes began to glow. His cock rose as well. "What I want is a passionate woman."

"Hmm," said Beth. She lay on her back and stretched, arms and legs wide. "Do you see any around?"

"Yep. There's one right here, ripe for the taking." He growled, rolled over her, and captured her mouth.

She tasted her own tang as his tongue fought hers. This is how their life would be, each of them fighting for control. Each of them giving in. She reveled in his power, completing the empty part of her and making her whole.

"What say you, Kate?" he said when they finally broke for air.

"Take me hard," she begged. "Make me yours."

With a feral growl, he rolled her over and pulled her to hands and knees. Like a stallion covering a mare, he grasped her hips and drove deep. Her body primed for so long, her heart singing, she screamed his name as she fell apart.

* * * *

"We're going behind the waterfall?"

Trace nodded at Beth. She'd never looked lovelier. Long strands of wet hair caressed her body. The sun sparkled off drops of water from their dip in the pool. The chilly water made her breasts hard and nipples harder.

"You see the lip of the waterfall?" He pointed to the flat plate where water spilled over. "It's a harder layer of rock than the face of the cliff."

"What's in there?"

"You asked if I paid in gold, like a miner."

"We were playing."

He held out his hand to her. She grasped his and he showed her where to step to avoid slipping. As the rock sides curved into the curtain of water, there was no way of knowing anything but a hard rock face existed behind.

He'd found the hidden meadow when his parents still lived. No one else knew of the meadow, much less his treasure. He stepped through the pounding water, towing Beth behind him. As soon as they were in, he pulled her body against his. He was used to cold far more than Beth.

"Oh, that was chilling," she said.

"But worth it." He kissed her nose. "Look around, but be careful you don't trip. The constant flow of water breaks off rocks all the time."

Rubbing her arms with her hands, she turned in a circle. Everything from small boulders to gravel covered the floor. He watched her reactions, knowing what was to come. He knew she'd be surprised, but what else?

"Ouch!" She winced and lifted her foot.

"Why don't you look at what you stepped on?"

She frowned at him. "I know that look. You're hiding something from me."

He pointed to the floor. She sighed dramatically and crouched down. He gulped when she spread her knees wide to balance while facing him. She picked up a handful of small rocks, glanced at them, and tossed them aside. After a second her mouth dropped open. She turned to where they landed and scrabbled around.

"I swear one of those rocks looked golden."

She scooped up a double handful and looked closely and then gulped. When her face lifted to his, her eyes were wide. Not in greed but awe.

"You left all this gold, just lying here?" She let it sift from between her fingers.

"It's not going anywhere. But I wanted you to know about this place. If we're blessed with children, they may need it someday."

"How many years has it been since you came here?"

"Last time was after I lived through this." He rubbed his throat.

"I don't know why you didn't die."

"Too stubborn."

"Tell me the truth."

He shrugged as if it meant nothing. "I couldn't die. Simon and Jack had nobody else. They were barely fourteen, still in shock from Ma and Pa dying. And I couldn't put two more onto the MacDougals."

"They must be wonderful people to take in four children when they already had seven. You've never told me the whole story."

He nodded. "When gold fever struck, they stood it as long as they could, wanting to keep us all together. But Fin and Sunbird like their space and there wasn't enough of it here. Soon as I was better, I hauled a few loads down the mountain and handed it over. Seven years ago they hauled everyone but Fin Junior, Hugh and Gillis to the Texas Hill Country and set up the Bar MD brand. Ross and Nevin came back four years ago to join Gillis. The other two lit out for Texas as soon as they could. I gave them a sack of nuggets to help pay the way."

Beth brushed off her hands and stood up. She washed the grit off in the water pounding past them. When she turned to him he saw a light in her eyes that made his heart ache.

"You are a wonderful man, Trace Elliott. Take me home."

"What about the gold?"

She shrugged and held out her arms. "I've got three Elliotts of my own. Why do I need gold?"

He wrapped his arms around her and held tight. He hadn't known this was a test until she passed it. If his face was wet, it came from the waterfall, nothing else.

Chapter Seventeen

"We should blindfold her first."

"She won't open her eyes until we tell her. Right, Beth?

Beth looked from Jack, who didn't trust her, to Simon, who did. Their reactions suited their distinct characters. Jack grinned openly while Simon lifted a corner of his mouth. His eyes, however, glowed. Whatever was going on, they were proud of themselves.

"What did the two of you do while we rode up the mountain?"

"Go upstairs and find out."

"I haven't gone up there since I found a pile of clothes that must have been moldering since you were children."

"They're gone."

"Did you open the windows? The place stank of onions and worse."

"Kate, move that sweet ass up those stairs before I paddle it!"

Trace's voice rose with each word. She looked from one man to the next and the last. All three twitched with eagerness, just like the puppies when she held a bone.

When they arrived home, Simon insisted on caring for Peaches while she had a nap. While they shared a light supper of soup and lightly scorched biscuits, the men often nudged each other and cleared their throats. The dogs had been sent to the barn for the evening though it was still light.

"That's it!" Trace approached her with a wild look in his eyes. He leaned his shoulder against her hip, grabbed her legs and stood up. She folded in half, her head hanging down his back.

"Put me down!" She grabbed his belt to hold herself secure.

"Nope. Keep your head down."

She shrieked, pounded him, and kicked, but it was like hitting rock.

"Hold it," said Jack. He grabbed one of her feet and started undoing her boot laces. Simon took the other. Her stockings soon followed, pulled off without any attempt to arouse. When she was barefoot Trace, swatted her bottom and started up the stairs.

Because she faced Trace's backside, she couldn't see anything until he swung her around and set her on her feet. A bit dizzy, she grabbed his arms until the room steadied.

"Oh, my."

They'd hung the set of four beautiful picture quilts Prudence MacDougal had given her. Pru had created the Elliott side of the valley out of fabric scraps. Beth had seen the view herself when looking out Pru's parlor window. A pair hung on each side of the center window that lit the northeast half of the open second floor. Winter's stark white, gray, and evergreens hung to the left beside spring's bright green with wildflowers. Summer's gold, sage green, and brown along with autumn's fiery show lit up the right side. They'd also hung a small picture frame above the window, though it seemed to be empty. She dropped her eyes past the window.

She gasped and stared.

One giant bed covered the floor except for narrow passages under the side eaves. She strained her head and looked again. Not one but three wide bed frames had their legs lashed together to create one huge surface. Each mattress had a clean white sheet tucked in all around. Four plump pillows rested against the wall. A matching number of faded quilts waited for night's chill. With three male furnaces burning, would she need quilts, even in January?

They'd placed her dressing table on the east wall. She'd never seen the cream and pink flowered wash bowl and matching water pitcher before. It must be for her personal use as she couldn't see the men touching that color. The silver-backed brush Trace loved to use on her lay next to a folded towel.

A series of carved pegs set in a board at her shoulder height held her dresses. A sea chest padded with a quilt provided a seat. A folded screen of woven grasses cut across the south corner. She sighed in relief. Even with one husband, a woman may want to change or do what was necessary without male eyes watching every move. Three pairs of them would be too much.

The room was to be shared, all right. Pegs set in a zigzag pattern held shirts and pants she recognized, having washed them often enough.

Simon and Jack must have moved the furniture in while she and Trace went up the mountain, but when had they scrubbed the floors and walls? It must have been when she and Trace visited Prudence and Gillis MacDougal the other week. She'd either been home or with two or more of them the rest of the time.

In this room, Trace, Simon, and Jack had made a family nest. They wanted her to sleep with them, to share the midnight murmurings that brought loving adults close together. Their time together at the waterfall was a gift, a few short hours to remember, like a honeymoon before returning to care for the whole family.

Trace understood. She wasn't just his wife. She was the woman they wanted to share their lives. She inhaled to feel the blood rushing through her pounding heart. She pressed her hand to her chest but it didn't ease her agitation. It wasn't love, but it was far more than she'd expected.

She'd stepped onto the Bride Train in Philadelphia determined to make it on her own. Weeks later, she stepped off in Dillon, her illusions shattered. Passing through Bannack City only strengthened her resolve not to give in and accept husbandly dregs. That first night, Trace showed her some of the advantages of marriage when all she'd known were negatives.

The twins soon engulfed her with their humor, passion, and determination. Yet, as Trace's wife, she'd not felt a full part of the

Rocking E. Knowing all three wanted her womanly comfort eased her heart. Not love, but affection and caring. More than most wives ever had.

"We kept the bed downstairs for you in case you're feeling poorly," said Simon.

"If Sy snores, we'll ship him off to sleep with Tony and Cleo in the barn," said Jack.

"I don't snore. And you'd better keep your ass tight and not let 'em rip after you've been into the beans."

She bit her lip to stop smiling. By building this room with one large bed, Trace said she belonged to all of them. Giving her a bed of her own elsewhere let her have privacy if she wanted it. That would be the bed she used to bring the next generation into the world. She did *not* want anyone else to see this room unless they, too, shared their men. If Amelia arrived and, God forbid, Pru died, there'd be two wives living with the same set of values, ones suited to the far western part of Montana Territory. The Bride Train may bring others, women who would understand how joy shared, was multiplied.

She pressed both hands over her face to stifle a hysterical giggle as the twins argued behind her. She'd never known siblings could be so ornery yet still care about each other. It was one of the things she loved about them. Honest and open, full of loud criticism, and quiet praise.

"Me? Dammit, Sy, you're the one who damn near crisped his butt setting fire to your stink."

"You said we'd be like dragons, only shooting backwards."

She tried to stop her shoulders shaking, but it was no good.

"You like it, sweetheart?"

She blinked rapidly, but a few tears spilled over her fingers.

"Dang it, Jack," said Trace. "Look at her shake. You're making her cry!"

She turned around to face them, her hands covering her cheeks. Trace was the first to notice her happy tears. His shoulders relaxed and he winked. Simon and Jack continued to argue with each other until Trace loudly cleared his throat. They turned to her.

She slid her palms over her cheeks, letting them see her smile.

"She likes it?"

She nodded. "Now I can hug all of you, all night if I want."

"You know, these mattresses are fresh," said Jack. He sent her his best leer. "They haven't been tried out yet. You must be tired after all that riding. Maybe you should lie down."

"I had a nap before supper."

"Then you won't mind staying awake for a bit," said Simon.

"Try it out," said Trace.

She could feel their puppy-like eagerness for her praise. She strolled forward. The floor had been well scrubbed. After years of boots, the boards were smooth under her bare feet. She tentatively settled on the edge of the bed at the far right.

"Seems sturdy," she said. Her words drew all three men toward her like a magnet. She stood on the mattress, her head above them for once. "It's a bit big for just me." She took a step back each time they moved forward. None of the men wore shoes or socks. They'd unbuttoned their shirts when she wasn't looking.

"Want some company?" said Trace. He shrugged his shoulders and his shirt slid to the floor.

"I wouldn't want to interrupt your plans for the evening. Weren't you in the middle of a checkers challenge with Jack? You'd each won two games in the best three out of five."

"Checkers?" Jack's shirt fell to the floor. "Why play a child's game when there's a bed to rumple?"

"We could put the board on her belly. See who can concentrate," suggested Simon.

Beth jumped when Jack's belt landed on the floor with a thunk. "What's the prize?" he asked. He scratched the hair below his belly button. His fingers drew Beth's eyes. She knew what waited behind that denim.

"I say the lady's the prize," replied Simon. He shucked his pants. His long cock aimed at her. He nonchalantly grasped it and slowly pumped, forward and back, as it grew.

"Nobody move," growled Trace. He strode across the room and down the stairs.

Beth, body heating under her clothing, looked from one eager man to the other. Jack tossed his pants aside, and then two men aimed their naked intentions at her. As ordered, no one took a step closer until Trace returned, checkers box in his hand. He set it on the sea chest and quickly stripped.

"Who's black?"

"I won the last game," said Simon.

"So I go first," said Jack. "Who gets to help our table get naked? Me and Sy did all the work setting it up, so I think we should. I'll take west."

Jack circled the bed and climbed up on her right side. Simon did the same to her left. Trace sauntered forward to the foot of the bed. He stood with feet apart, shoulders set, and arms crossed. His dark nest of hair sprouted a massive handle. If she needed help climbing down from the bed, he wouldn't have to offer his arm. His third leg looked sturdy enough.

Jack, ever the rake, picked up her right hand and bent over. He kissed her knuckles as if they met in a city soiree and she wore white gloves past her elbows. Instead, he turned over her hand and kissed the calluses already growing on her work-roughened hands.

Simon picked up her left hand and, wasting no time, flicked a wrist button open. He turned her hand over and grazed the sensitive spot under her cuff, right where her palm ended. She stood, arms out as if in benediction until they finished with her sleeves.

"I'll start at the top buttons," said Simon.

Before Jack could react, he brushed a knuckle over her cheek and tilted her chin up. His shoulder brushed her swelling breast as his fingers worked to free her throat. Jack sank to his knees in front of her. He tugged her blouse out of her waistband. He'd unbuttoned past her belly before Simon passed her breasts.

They raced to reach the last and flung her blouse behind her. Instead of cooling from removing the confining fabric, heat rushed through her, filling her tight breasts. A set of soft lips suckled each one. She reached behind to brace herself against the wall, closing her eyes to the sensation. She shivered when fingers trailed down her belly to her skirt. Someone undid the few skirt buttons and it dropped to her feet.

They helped her to lie on her back across the bed. Trace set the checkers board so one edge grazed her breasts and the other rested on her hip bones. He set up the pieces, black for Jack and red for Simon. They sat with crossed ankles on each side of her. The board, wider than she, hid their fingers when they caressed her from her ribs to hips. She twitched at the tickle.

"Hands to yourselves," said Trace. He lifted her head on a pillow and settled there, his knees framing her ears. Smiling down at her, he began pulling out her pins and releasing her hair. He combed it with his fingers, draping it over the pillow and around him.

She relaxed, the center of their attention. For once the twins played in silence rather than tormenting each other. When she first arrived, she thought they behaved like giant undisciplined children. Once she'd shared herself with them and the initial tension was gone, she realized it was their belligerent male way of showing they cared about each other. Trace would grouse and they'd give back just as strong. She'd learned to read their bodies and tone of voice rather than the words they threw around.

Though a huge man played with her hair and two more snuggled tight against her sides, she was the most relaxed of them. Checkers was just a game to her. It didn't matter who kissed her first as soon all four of them would be participating. But to the twins, everything was a contest. Perhaps now that they would share a bed all night, they would feel more secure.

Jack hopped three of Simon's pieces, the sound loud on the wooden board. Simon hissed a curse and Jack snorted a laugh. She smiled up at Trace. He lifted his eyebrows in question. She mouthed *I'm happy* to him. He tugged gently on her hair to show he understood.

The board tickled the underside of her breasts, making her quiver. Jack, halfway through a move with one hand lifted, stared at her trembling flesh. A snort from Simon and he completed his move. Simon immediately snapped up two of the black disks and tossed them aside. He tapped the board for Jack to "king" him.

"Whose side you on?" said Jack.

"Mine," Beth replied. "The board is getting a bit heavy."

Jack and Simon looked at each other. As far as Beth could tell, no words were spoken. But both hooted at the same time. One swept the checkers wide while the other lifted the board and tossed it toward the foot of the bed.

"Heads," said Jack.

"Tails," replied Simon.

Jack rose to his knees. He leaned over her and, with an enormous sigh, settled his lips over her left nipple. Simon bent her knees and pressed them apart. He encouraged her to lift her bottom and pushed a pillow under. He lay on his stomach between her thighs. He gently kissed the inside of her thigh, then slid his tongue between her pussy lips.

Beth arched her back. She thrust her breasts toward Jack and tilted herself toward Simon.

"Heads and tails," whispered Trace. "Either way, you win."

* * * *

Trace shifted to the side not occupied by Jack and lay down, resting his head on his fist. Eyes closed and mouth wide, Beth gasped as Jack and Simon tried to outdo each other in driving her wild. With room to spread out, they could finally treat her right. While he'd enjoyed having Beth to himself, a part of him knew it wasn't right. They'd never say anything, but his brothers needed to hold Beth tight in the night just as much as he.

Before he'd given up on finding a wife, he'd thought one would be a convenience. He'd get meals, a clean house and clothes, and sex. In return he'd have to put up with a female clinging to him. He wasn't sure why he thought that, since Ma clung to no one. Maybe it was the married women he saw in town, Bannack City, or Dillon. They'd swish past him in their fancy dresses, making sure a big, dirty brute like him never came close.

The first time he saw Beth, going nose to nose with Charlie, he'd realized she was not like the town women. Good thing, too. She inhaled a gasp, trembled and moaned. Simon and Jack looked up, grinned at each other and went back to pleasuring her.

Their woman.

Did his seed grow within her already? She had never turned him away for her woman time and there'd not been one night when they slept apart. A tight band shot around his chest. He sat up, fighting to breathe.

A father? Him?

He rubbed his front, knuckles pressing against the bone between his chest muscles. The pain eased, melting like snow in a winter chinook.

Maybe.

Trace, the oldest and ugliest of the Elliott brothers, might have a wife swelling with his babe. Did she know? He looked down at her, writhing under the fingers, tongues, and mouths of his twin little brothers.

"Oh, yes!"

She bucked and trembled, her skin glowing with sweat. When her storm began to ease, Jack rolled onto his back, full mast high. Sy lifted Beth, gently guiding her to settle around Jack. He caressed her breasts, rasping her nipples and making her moan. Simon brought over the sweet lard they'd prepared earlier and settled behind her. Jack encouraged her to shift forward, kissing her deep.

Trace moved to the side to watch Simon, making sure he was careful with Beth. As Jack was thick, it was best that Sy, more narrow and long, enter her ass. He watched her tight little asshole clench around Sy's fingers as he greased her up. The minx pushed back against him, demanding more. Trace joined in, playing with her sopping clit. Her need and moans grew. Simon slathered his cock well and rose to his knees. He splayed his hands and pressed her cheeks apart. Her little brown anus grew an inside pink ring as she relaxed for him.

Trace double-fingered her clit, twitching his fingers between her belly and Jack's. Sy guided his cock to her ass and pressed. She pushed back and he slid an inch, just inside her ring. He nodded to Jack, who encouraged Beth to slide down his cock and take him deep. Trace moved aside to watch Jack's thick cock disappear inside her. She then rose as Simon pumped slow and deep.

Cocks moved in and out as Beth slid forward on Jack and back on Sy. They sped up, Simon going deeper, faster. Beth, belly to Jack, scraped her clit on him with each stroke. Sy's balls slapped against her lips with every forward stroke.

Trace's cock tried to stiffen enough to join the fun, but he'd damn near killed himself earlier at the waterfall so he relaxed and watched the twins drive Beth wild. She tossed her head and her hair flew, striking Jack's face and chest when Simon slammed into her.

None of them noticed him watching. Sy's eyes were fixed on Beth's ass. Jack, hands guiding Beth's hips, stared at her face and breasts. Beth's eyes were jammed shut as she took whatever she wanted from his brothers.

Something triggered the explosion. Beth gasped and ground herself onto Jack with all her weight. Simon yelled something and slammed once more into her before his rhythm broke down and he quaked like he was having a fit. Just as Simon finished, Jack erupted, lifting and dropping Beth onto him, Sy attached, until he, too groaned. Beth collapsed over him, Simon lying over her like a sopping blanket.

Sy held Beth and rolled sideway, taking her, and Jack with him.

Instead of being excluded, Trace felt he was part of the action. After tonight, Beth would need some time to recover. He'd never thought that one naked woman falling asleep on his chest would do more for him than a bed full of lively whores. Not that he'd ever had such a thing, nor did he want to anymore.

He slipped down to the kitchen to get the kettle, still warm from the stove. He brought an old towel with him, tossing it to an exhausted Simon when he pulled out. He filled the ewer and wet the soft cloth the boys put out earlier. Gently, he bathed the sweat off Beth's back and bottom. She murmured when he lifted her off Jack and laid her on her back. More warm water tidied up her top side.

She had a silly little girl smile, one that he cherished. It meant she was so far beyond caring about things, that all she knew was pleasure.

He set her in the center of the bed and covered her with a soft quilt. She curled on her side, still smiling. Jack quirked an eyebrow at him but he shook his head. The boys had earned it. They'd sleep on either side of Beth tonight.

Sy curled up behind her, cupping her upper breast in his hand. He shuddered a sigh and relaxed. How long had it been since his middle brother had felt so content?

Jack, still the ladies' man, faced toward Beth. He settled farther down in the bed, his lips almost touching her breasts.

Though they were warm now, it would soon get cooler. Trace covered each man with a quilt. He looked at them for a moment and then trod down the stairs, shaking his head. Huh! Imagine him, tucking up his little brothers after they drove his hot wife wild.

He threw on a pair of boots and headed out to the barn. He felt like his skin was too tight or something. He absently rubbed his chest. The pull to return to their bed was too strong. He couldn't let a physical need dominate his decisions. Beth was a good wife, and she'd make a good mother. She'd changed their lives for the better, but he didn't need her more than life.

Not like his father needed his mother. Never like that.

Beth was a damned fine convenience, one he'd cherish. But that was all.

The dogs greeted him with joyous tail wags. Sailor raised a sleepy head as if to ask what the hell he was doing in the barn at this hour.

Hell if he knew. But he couldn't go back into that bed and still be who he was, strong and alone, needing no one.

Chapter Eighteen

They came, as Beth expected, when Trace, Simon, and Jack were in the mountains chasing cattle.

She'd had a few weeks to practice her aim. With luck and a light wind she could hit the target with her rifle if it was braced on something. The pistol was another matter. Trace said she'd only be good at close quarters so she might as well hide it in her pocket.

He was joking but she listened. She sewed strong pockets in each dress, just the right size to hold the pistol and her hand. If anyone tried to take her, he'd get a bullet in his gut. After that, all the piece of iron was good for was whacking someone on the head. If she had to, she would.

Whenever the men went far, she kept her pistol in her pocket and rifle near. She'd just returned to the garden from the privy when Tony and Cleo alerted her with sharp yips that someone was coming up from the river. Three hard, dirty men approached riding tired, dusty horses they'd likely stolen.

She got in the house before they got too close, calling the dogs in with her. She set her pistol on the table, grabbed the freshly loaded rifle and knelt to watch through the open kitchen window as they approached. Tony shoved at her arm, making space for his front paws on the window ledge to watch. Cleo whined low in her throat as she paced back and forth between the window and the door.

Tony turned his head to Beth, licked her chin, and went back on guard duty. Beth's stomach roiled with acid, a reminder of what had happened the last few mornings. They'd headed out early, leaving her still asleep. She hadn't eaten anything different from the men, who showed no signs of sickness.

Perhaps it was the heat this last week. It made her so drowsy she rested on the downstairs bed for an hour during the worst of the afternoon heat. How would she cope in July and August if she was this weak now? She'd just have to toughen up. After she got rid of these ruffians.

"Don't come any closer or I'll shoot," she yelled when their horses had approached close enough to the house that she had a decent chance of hitting one. Tony, as if adding his two cents, growled and snarled beside her. They pulled up about fifteen feet from where she knelt at the kitchen window.

"There's three of us, Miz Elliott, and your men folk are far away."

The pot-bellied man in a sweat-stained vest leered at her, revealing brown teeth. The one to her right, barely old enough to have a beard shadow, hung back. The other resembled the leader's features, though he was muscular rather than running to fat. He stared at her with cold, hungry eyes. She cocked the rifle. The leader lifted both hands in a conciliatory gesture.

"Now, don't get riled. We just wanna little visit."

Trace had instructed Beth to shoot first and ask questions later. She braced herself and slid the rifle out the kitchen window, resting it on the ledge. The man on the left snickered while the young one backed his horse up a few steps. She shoved Tony away with her elbow. He ran to the door with Cleo, both of them barking.

Bracing for the recoil, she aimed, closed her eyes, and fired.

The blast knocked her shoulder back, and she almost fell over. Her ears rang, the noise being far greater inside the house than out behind the barn. She heard screams over the sound of her dogs. When she got back in position the man on the left lay on the ground, clutching his left chest. His horse had bolted. The boss and young man fought to settle their horses as bright red blood pumped into her yard. It seemed only a moment before the body stopped moving.

Beth gulped and turned to the leader. The man had no idea she'd aimed for him and hitting the other was a lucky shot. She trembled and fought her heaving stomach.

"Dayam! You kilt Dan'l!" The leader lifted his pistol at her. "You'll pay for that, Miz Elliott. To hell with Big Joe. I'm gonna take you for myself."

Though she shivered at his words, she glared at him, the rifle giving her strength.

"Yep," he continued, "you'll bring a heap of gold when we're finished with ya." He spit in her direction but spoke to his side-kick. "Bet she takes two men regular."

Beth aimed at the leader again and fired. This time she kept her eyes open and managed to nick his horse. It screamed and reared in the air. The rider fought to hold and settle the horse but it bucked him off. The man landed heavily, grunting as he hit. The horse followed its herd mate past the barn.

The young man, face pale, shook his head at Beth. "You said we was just to scare her. I ain't a part of this no more," he said. He reined his horse around and took off at a fast trot for the river.

Eyes fixed on Beth, the leader hauled himself to his feet. When he straightened he looked almost as tall as Trace. The wind blew toward her, bringing his acrid stench. She gulped to keep her stomach contents where they were. He took a step forward. The dogs, knowing someone was outside, scratched madly at the door, howling. The bandit cocked his gun at her.

"Your bullets are gone, Miz Elliott. Get your ass out here or I'll shoot your dogs right through that door."

"No, please don't hurt my puppies!" She cried, pretending to be hysterical. It wasn't difficult. She prayed that Trace and the twins weren't far. But if she had to do this by herself, then she would. Somehow, she would survive with body and soul intact.

"Git out here. Now!"

She rose to her feet with the help of a quaking hand braced on the window sill. She placed her hot rifle on the table and set her pistol in the deep right pocket she'd sewn in her skirt. She pulled out hairpins to let her long blonde hair down to catch his attention.

She pulled the door open, fighting to get through and keep the dogs inside. They weaseled around her and raced outside, barking madly. Blonde hair gleaming in the sun, she stood in the doorway. She put her right hand in her pocket with her pistol and cried for him not to hurt her precious dogs as she checked his height. If she aimed the pistol up just a bit, she'd hit him in the belly.

"Git down here!" he roared. "Now!"

She nodded, blinking as if to hold back tears and gripped her weapon. She fluttered her other hand over her chest. She stepped out her front door and approached him with baby steps, down the few stairs and past her flower garden. She kept her shoulders back, shaking as if crying. He held his gun in his right hand and watched her approach. She held skirt with her left hand, her right still clutching the gun in her pocket. She stopped just far enough away so he couldn't reach her. She shook her head so her hair floated around her shoulders.

He watched her, his gun drooping toward the dirt, and then motioned her forward.

She took the last step, aimed for the middle of his belly, and pulled the trigger. Both guns went off. Propelled backward by the recoil, Beth landed on her bottom in the front garden. Something prickly scratched her back.

Her assailant curled into a ball, screaming like a banshee, high and wild as he attempted to hold his stomach together. Beth shoved her pistol back in her pocket. The bandit rolled, one arm flailing for his pistol. She scrabbled forward on her knees and grabbed it. She stood, backing away as the dogs danced around her, barking. She stepped on something and almost tripped.

The dead man's hand. Beth screamed and threw the bandit's pistol far away. She ran into her house with her dogs, away from the macabre scene, and barred the door. Only then did her pounding heart and trembles begin to slow. Through the kitchen window she watched the man writhe, still making horrid noises. She turned away and leaned against the wall, hissing as sharp pains bit into her back.

She pulled her gun out of her pocket and sank to the floor. She gathered her quivering dogs to each side of her, praising them and waited for the bandit to stop moving.

When she heard crows flying close to investigate, she figured the men were dead enough. She slowly got to her feet. She watched out the window for a few minutes but nothing moved. She brought cool water into her bedroom, stripped down and washed herself off. She put on the white and pink dress Trace had bought her the morning after their wedding. She took her bloody clothes to the kitchen and set them to soak in cold water.

Gathering up her courage she unbarred the door and walked out. She would not hide in the house like a silly Eastern woman. She was now a woman of the West, strong and brave. Even if her entire body shook with the remnants of terror, she would do what was necessary.

The dogs whined, warning her once more. She reached for her empty pistol but it was only a riderless horse approaching the barn. Avoiding the bodies littering her yard, she focused her attention on the animal. Its sides heaved with every deep breath. She walked toward it making a crooning sound, then reached out and grasped the reins. She looked up into the liquid black eyes of a bay.

"Aren't you a beauty?"

Grateful for something to do, Beth brought the horse to the far side of the barn and tied it there. She stripped off the saddle and blanket. The horse shook itself out, rippling its skin. She took what she needed from the barn and wiped it down. She focused on the needs of the horse rather than what waited in the yard. Keeping her hands busy kept her from running to the mountains and Trace, screaming her fear.

She groomed the delighted animal with long, soothing strokes. Hearing a horse blow, she turned to find the leader's horse, reins dangling. Her bullet had grazed its flank, scoring the flesh but not too deeply.

"I'm sorry, I hit you," she crooned. "Come here and I'll make it better." The bay nickered and walked forward.

Beth kept her mind blank as she worked on the second horse. The two dogs panted in the sun beside the corner of the barn. Tony faced the mountains while Cleo kept an eye on her. She knew their senses were far more acute than hers but every few minutes she looked up, hoping to spot a trail of dust descending toward her.

* * * *

Trace pushed his horse faster than was good for either of them. If they made it home to find Beth safe, without either of them breaking a leg or worse, the gelding would have nothing but hot mash the rest of its life.

"Beth!"

He screamed as loud as his broken voice box allowed. The wind blew up the mountain so there was no way she could hear him, but he wasn't thinking. Uneasy, he'd turned for home a few minutes before he heard a rifle shot. The second, a few minutes later, sped him up. They told Beth to give two shots, a few minutes apart, if there was trouble. He had a ten minute lead on Simon and Jack, minutes that might save Beth.

Big Joe hadn't been to town for a few weeks, but that meant nothing. He could be holed up anywhere between here and Virginia City. On top of that, Sheldrake was too lazy to do his own work. He'd hire someone who couldn't be traced back to him.

Halfway home, he saw a man trotting his horse toward the river. Trace's keen eyes spotted an unmoving man lying flat in the yard in front of the house. Beth had actually shot one? He bared his teeth in something between a grin and grimace. As he descended and the land flattened, the back of the house shielded him from what was happening out front.

His heart almost stopped at the double pistol shot. The cold and pain of Hell hit him as if the bullet had pierced his heart. Was Beth dead?

No. She couldn't be. God would not do that to him.

Please, I could have died many times. You must have saved me for something. If I am to die saving Beth, my life will have had meaning.

Without Beth, there was little reason to live. She brought life, light, and laughter to his miserable existence.

He'd sworn he'd never love a woman as much as his father did his mother. Trace ate those words with every pounding hoof as he raced home to the woman of his heart.

"Beth!"

His horse took the corner of the house like a born cattle horse. Trace leaped off his back and stared around wildly.

Two dead men. No Beth.

He ran toward the house. The rose bush he'd shipped from back East was crushed. Beth loved that rose.

Her dogs sped from the barn, barking like mad fools. They danced around him for a moment then ran back silently, turning their heads to see if he followed, tongues hanging.

"Sweetheart? Where are you?"

He almost beat the dogs to the far side of the barn. Beth stood with a pair of unfamiliar horses, curry comb in hand. His heart stopped for a moment before pounding even harder. He blinked to clear his tears.

"Trace?"

Her shaking voice, the most wondrous sound he'd ever heard, reached out and clutched his heart. He swooped her into his arms, both laughing and crying.

"Ouch, my back! Put me down!"

"You're alive, Beth!"

"I won't be if you squish me any harder."

"Oh, God, Beth, I'm sorry."

Careful of her back, he held her tight to his chest, his heart pounding, blood louder than his rasping breath.

"I don't know what I would have done if you...Are you..." He couldn't say the words. "They didn't—"

"I'm fine. They didn't." She smiled, though it wobbled. "I managed to get close enough to shoot him without him touching me." She shuddered. "I killed two men. Oh, my God, I'm going to be sick!"

She tried to pull away. He carried her beside the horse trough. She retched, the same as she had that morning. He gently cared for her then brought her a dipper full of fresh water.

The dogs set up another round of barking as Simon and Jack came around the corner and scrambled off their lathered horses. Beth took one look at them and burst into tears.

"She's okay," whispered Trace, unable to even croak. He kissed her forehead, her face, anywhere he could reach.

"Great," gasped Jack, his shaking voice proving his concern. "The cavalry arrives and the fair maiden breaks into tears."

Beth held out her arms. Trace released her so that Jack and Simon could hold her.

"Careful of my back. I landed on my rose bush."

They carefully hugged her, blinking hard.

"You did a damn fine job," said Simon, choking out the words.

"I killed them," she wailed.

"Better them than you," said Jack. "Come on, Sy, let's walk the horses." He caught the reins of Trace's lathered horse and, along with Simon, walked the animals to cool them down.

"I love you, Beth," whispered Trace.

"You're just glad I'm alive," said Beth. "It'll pass."

"No." Trace shook his head. "I finally realized what my father meant when he said he loved my mother."

He pressed a finger against her mouth when she tried to speak.

"My parents died of a fever. Ma was still pretty sick when Pa started to get better. They were in the same bed, together as they'd always been. When Ma got worse, Pa said he couldn't live without her. That he loved her so much, life was empty without her. They both died that night. Holding hands."

"Oh, Trace."

"I swore I'd never love anyone like that. No woman would have such power over me that I'd give my life for hers."

He lifted her chin and gently kissed her lips.

"I was wrong, Beth. I love you. Just as my father and mother, I'd give my life for you." He dropped his forehead to rest it against hers. He ignored the tears rolling down his cheeks to blend with hers.

"Forever, Beth. That's how long I'll love you. But don't, for God's sake, make me choose between you and our children." He kissed her gently once. Twice. "Damn, woman!"

* * * *

"Don't it make you want to cry," muttered Simon as he watched Trace tenderly kissing Beth's eyes. He couldn't hear what Trace said, but he could lips read well enough to know Trace said the L-word.

"Looks like big brother finally admitted what we've known all along," continued Simon. "'Bout time. Now we can do the same."

"I guess he gets first dibs at her since he's her husband," groused Jack half-heartedly.

"Great. He gets to bury himself in Beth's hot body while we clean up the yard."

"Did you see the new horses? Must belong to the guys Beth beefed."

"Wonder what was in their saddlebags."

"Stolen gold, you think?"

"Do we check or bring them to the sheriff as they are?"

Simon raised an eyebrow. "Let Frank go through their pockets."

"There's an old canvas tarp in the barn. We can use that to carry them in the wagon. I'll lift the feet."

"I think I saw pictures of both of these men hanging in the jail. Maybe we'll get a reward."

"Let's surprise Beth with some new rose bushes," said Jack.

"We'd be better off using it as a reward."

"I'll have a word with Frank. He can let Sheriff Plummer know anyone even thinking of hurting Beth will have every Elliott and MacDougal hounding him to Hell."

"I wouldn't want Nevin or Ross on my tail." Simon snorted and shook his head. "I swear those boys can read the sign of the wind and leave no trail a white man can follow. If someone hurt a woman they cared about, dying would be a relief."

Finished in the barn, they followed Beth's voice outside. Beth, stark naked, had her arms wrapped around Trace.

"When do you think she'll be ready to celebrate our helping to save her, even if we did arrive a bit late?"

"Trace was late, too," said Simon.

"Good point."

"Hey, what about my hero's welcome?" called Jack.

"Had to check my wife for injuries," said Trace when Simon frowned. "The recoil from the pistol knocked her into the rose bush."

"Yep, I heard rose thorns can be dangerous," said Simon. "We'd best make sure none are stuck in you."

Trace turned to Beth. "Sy, Jack, I love this woman."

"So do we," said Simon. "Took you long enough to figure it out."

"He must have bashed his head one too many times getting towed behind that horse," said Jack to Simon.

Trace lifted Beth into his arms.

"Put me down! Trace, what are you doing?"

He turned in a circle with her in his arms, around and around, laughing.

"No! You'll make me sick again!"

"Better listen to her," said Jack. "She looks pretty white. Or maybe green."

Trace stopped and set her feet down. She dropped to her knees, gasping and holding her belly.

"What's the matter, sweetheart?" Trace rubbed her back.

"This happen before you shot those bandits, Beth?" asked Simon.

She nodded. "I think I ate something bad. The last couple of mornings I felt miserable, but it went away." She took Simon's hand and stood up. She frowned and stared at the ground as if thinking hard.

"Trace, Beth's been awful tired lately. I came home to change horses and found her in your old bed yesterday. She never even knew I went by."

"We'll take her into town first thing in the morning," said Trace. "If the doc isn't around, Miss Lily might know what's the matter."

Simon looked at Jack. Jack's lip twitched. Simon snorted. Jack slapped Trace on the back.

"Wait until we tell Miss Lily that we figured it out before the bridegroom," said Simon. They were fifteen when Trace was injured. Refusing to leave him, they'd lived with Miss Lily for the few weeks Trace was bedridden. Among other things, they'd learned how to spot the early stages of pregnancy. A lesson that Trace had obviously missed.

"You really don't know, do you, bro?"

Trace grabbed the front of Jack's shirt and hauled him on to his toes. "Tell me what's so funny. Now!"

Beth pulled at Simon's arm. "Do you think I might be growing a baby?"

Since Trace's hands were full of Jack, Simon drew her close to him. He wrapped his arms around her and inhaled deep. Only then did he step back and kiss her forehead.

"Yep. You'd best start knitting, Beth. Tiny things."

Beth gasped. She pressed a hand on her lower belly. A smile wider than Montana appeared on her face. Trace, watching her dawning comprehension, shoved Jack away. He held out trembling arms to Beth.

"Oh, sweetheart! I wanted to believe but wasn't sure."

Jack, smile wide, smoothed his shirt front as he watched Trace and Beth kiss.

"We're gonna be uncles, Sy."

"Next one's mine," said Simon. "I want a sweet little blonde-haired girl like Beth."

"Mine'll be a boy," replied Jack. "Unless it's one of each."

"Excuse me." They turned to Beth. "May I have one baby before you decide on more?"

Jack and Simon looked at each other. They shrugged and then turned to Beth. "Whatever the momma wants," said Jack. "Miss Lily said her girls get all hot and bothered once the morning sickness passes. Then they want to scratch their itch pretty bad."

"You feel itchy, Beth?" asked Simon.

Beth lifted her head from Trace's chest. "I don't know about itchy, but I need some loving and a long nap. It's been a very long day."

Trace placed one hand behind Beth's back, another behind her knees, and lifted her into his arms once more. He turned and started walking toward the house.

"You didn't tell me you were feeling poorly," said Trace. "That's one. You scared the hell out of me. That's two. This daddy thing, well, that's number three. I've been meaning to spank you for some time. Racing down that mountain I realized things can't wait. So I decided today's the day, wife."

"What? Simon, Jack, help me!"

Simon knew that any spanking Beth received would be gentle love pats, but he'd let her discover that for herself. Struggling in Trace's loving arms would help release the tension in her muscles from the afternoon's ordeal.

"Afternoon, ma'am," he said, lifting his hat as she passed.

"Nice ass you got there," said Jack.

"It is nice," said Trace. He stopped, letting them catch up. "Feel how soft her skin is, right there."

Jack took the initiative and slid his fingers between her thighs, drawing out her nectar with a rough finger. He licked his finger. "She's ripe all right."

Trace winked at his brothers. "You helped save her. Want to help paddle her?"

"No!" Beth squealed and kicked. The men laughed, more in relief than at her predicament. "Let me go!"

"Not until we're finished with you." Trace's smile was wide. "Right, boys?"

"We'd better wash her off and rub something into those scratches first," said Simon.

"I guess it's time to haul out that new copper bathtub I ordered."

"You got the bathtub?" Beth stopped struggling.

"I'll fire up the stove and fill the reservoir," said Jack.

"Set the tub by the kitchen door in the sun," ordered Trace. "We'll have to check every inch of her to make sure there's nothing sticking in her."

"Nothing but us, you mean."

"I know what we can rub into those scratches, Beth."

Trace slowed to let his brothers set things up. When they were alone, he held her tight and dropped his head onto hers.

"This has been the worst and best day of my life," he whispered.

"I was so scared when I saw those men ride up."

"But you did what you had to do." Trace kissed her forehead. "I knew you were the woman for me. Strong and proud. I do love my wild barefoot bride."

She wiggled her toes. "That's not all that's bare."

"Saves me ripping all those buttons off again."

"I love you, Trace Elliott. And I love your brothers, too."

"Good. We're going to be together for a long, long time."

He followed the sound of Simon and Jack's squabbling as they fought over who would get to wash Beth, to kiss her, and to drive deep inside her.

He hugged her tight, knowing the answer was simple. All three of them would love her, forever.

THE END

www.ReeceButler.net

ABOUT THE AUTHOR

Reece Butler lives outside a large city just far enough to commute to her full-time job, yet come home to the quiet countryside. While her hardworking husband and sons are proud of her, they do miss the baking and special things she used to do before writing erotic romance took over her so-called spare time.

She takes her research seriously and recently returned from a week at a dude ranch learning how to be a cowboy. She gained a few bruises, sore muscles and learned about feeding, riding, roping and cleaning up after horses. Wranglers, and cowboys, are up before dawn to get the grain buckets ready and last feeding is late in the evening. Fantasy cowboy life is far easier than reality!

Reece then spent a couple weeks conducting in-depth research while driving around southwest Montana where this fictional erotic romance series is set.

There is, unfortunately, no room in her life for a horse. However, fantasy fills the gaps and in her dreams she rides Dee-Dee, the Arabian bay mare, up the trail to view the sunset on a Tennessee evening.

Also by Reece Butler

Cowboy Combo 1: *Cowboy Sandwich*
Cowboy Combo 2: *Cowboy Double-Decker*

Siren Publishing, Inc.
www.SirenPublishing.com

Breinigsville, PA USA
27 November 2010
250162BV00007B/2/P